WOMEN CALLED
So ARISE

The scepter shall not depart from Judah, Nor a lawgiver from between His feet: Genesis 49:10a

With the scepter in her hand - The Sword of the Spirit, the word of God in her mouth; Ephesians 4:17b, and the Lion of Judah by her side, 'WOMEN CALLED So ARISE' are fearless, exercise authority with the weapons of Faith, Hope, and Love.

For the scepter of righteousness is the scepter of Your kingdom: Psalm 45:6b

For the scepter of wickedness shall not rest on the land allotted to the righteous, lest the righteous reach out their hands to iniquity: Psalm 125:3

Cynderella Helen Handwatch

Unless otherwise indicated, all Scripture quotations are taken from the Holy Bible - New King James Version

National Library of New Zealand
ISBN 978-0-473-48981-6

CONTENTS

TRAILBLAZERS

-

PREFACE

The novel *His Eye Upon Us features Sasha and Veronique.*
Since escaping from their traffickers, they had become inseparable.
Through their experience, they established House of Destiny
(HOD), a Non-Profit Organisation-Transitional House. House of
Destiny assisted abused women and children, human trafficking
victims, rehabilitated and reintegrated them back into society.
Tireless in pursuit of the causes in which she believed, Sasha was
ready to embark on the next phase of her journey of life, The
Nehemiah Building Project (NBP). The concept inspired by the Book
of Nehemiah in the Bible, aimed at building people's lives.

"What happens now?" Veronique asked Sasha tentatively.
The previous night they had had a long discussion on the final
arrangements concerning NBP. Sasha, on the other hand, was quite
excited by the imminent trip. She felt confident Veronique would
be able to manage the NPO during her absence. Although
Veronique was skeptical, Sasha somehow was able to convince her
of her capability.

"Besides," said Sasha, "this venture is an integral part of the
ongoing program for the NBP. You are going to be kept quite busy,
so there won't be time to miss me."

"Well, as long as you are not going to run off and leave me
totally on my own, then I'm willing to give it a go," Veronique finally
agreed.

"Yes, Linda has promised to pop in now and then to give
you a hand." (Linda, Sasha's friend also featured in 'HIS EYE UPON
US.' Convinced Sasha kidnapped, she had hired the services of a
young detective to find her. Instead, the detective had fallen in
love with Sasha's captor. Ever since their escapade, Linda had kept
a watchful eye over the girls, knowing each time they took a risk
when assisting trafficked and abused women and children). "But
you still have to convince me. What makes you think that God

wants women to take on these tasks I feel have for centuries been male-dominated?" Veronique asked for the hundredth time.

And finally, Sasha had been obligated to once more expound on her findings on the research she had been doing.

These findings had motivated her to pursue the journey she was now undertaking.

"Well, as you know, I've been studying the accounts of certain women in the Bible. The sole purpose of their stories is to preserve God's truth. And I'm convinced they are written entirely for our benefit.

"And what truth is that?"

"That God enlisted women to do His work then, and that He still engages the services of women today. He's ushering in continues, evident in the accomplishment of women; women still giving life, still saving nations, and still judging and governing people. You understand why some of their stories have motivated me into undertaking this venture."

"Yes, now I know," said Veronique, sighing deeply as a tightness gripped her throat.

Sasha begins sharing her discoveries in chronological order. She opens her narrative with women in the Old Testament and concludes with women in the New Testament.

"Some of our renowned biblical characters are Eve, Achsah, the daughters of Zelophehad, Deborah, Naomi and Ruth, The Queen of Sheba, Mary and Elizabeth, to name just a few. I feel we must hold these women in high esteem. These are some of the women who we can emulate, for they have played a significant role in shaping the history of humankind since creation.

Besides the women of the Bible, many other women have ruled the continents. But the world seldom speaks of their achievements, struggles, and the challenges they've had to endure. Some have had a huge impact on the nations they ruled, but have a disproportionate impact on history worldwide because of their gender status. Many rose to power through fierce defiance in a male-dominated world. Their perseverance, resilience, and brilliance laid the foundation for the success of their nations and examples for the 21stcentury women to follow.

Gender inequality was prevalent back then as it is today. Being female rulers, many of the citizens had little faith in their ability to rule. Because of this mistrust, they had to work twice as hard to assure them that they could govern as well as men, if not better. Some not only encountered irrational opposition, but they ruled under dark shadows of doubt, suspicion, and hostile scrutiny.

Today because of democracy, human and women's rights advocacies, mindsets have been challenged, and society's perspective towards women taking the helm has changed. Without a doubt, it has provided unparalleled opportunities for women to ascend to pinnacles of success and power. Our current and historical female leaders set the trend for women's leadership empowerment. However, I believe the foundation had already been laid by our biblical women leaders. All we had to do was to follow their examples and use similar tenacities to accomplish that which we have been called to do.

I believe incredible and dynamic women full of the integrity of God are more than ready to fulfill their roles in society outside the confines of system constructed walls. Women from all walks of life, from every social sphere and at every level of academia, economic, and political arena, have solutions to the problems that beset all nations. These stalwarts hailing from every social background will bring in workable value-added solutions to the crises and challenges encountered in families, communities, cities, and nations as a whole."

"You make it sound so challenging and yet at the same time both dramatic and intriguing, especially after what we've been through," said Veronique.

"I guess it's always venturing into the unknown that's the challenge. But now that our faith has grown in leaps and bounds, and knowing who is leading us, it's merely taking a step of faith to do what He has called us to do. Besides, we've already been through so many challenges, and we survived. We'll survive this too," said Sasha.

"Today, there are still male-dominated institutes where inequity is observable as females work harder than their counterparts to prove their competency. In these environments, though better qualified, women are disadvantaged because of biases and prejudices. However, following one's purpose when answering God's pre-ordained call is merely the steering of ancient wheels that through obedience, sets into motion. Thankfully we no longer have to succumb to the whims, ideologies, and dictates of the worlds which would prohibit the fulfillment of God's plans. Once He gives the 'Green Light,' and you have the conviction in your heart, then it's time to 'Cross Over.'"

1

EVE

MOTHER OF ALL LIVING

Biblical women have played a significant role in shaping our lives, and we begin with the very first woman, Eve. The first divine, spiritual, and feminine life-giving sacred act of God's was infusing in Eve the ability to produce life from her womb. This life was through the reproduction cycle and union between male and female.

In the beginning, God placed Adam in the Garden of Eden to tend and care for it. He also gave Adam dominion over the earth and the supernatural ability to name all He had created. But, then, Adam hearkened to the voice of Eve, whom God had given him for companionship and as his helpmate. He disobeyed God's specific instruction not to eat the fruit from the tree of the knowledge of good and evil given to him by Eve. So the Lord God banished them from the Garden. However, just before being driven out of the Garden, Adam named the woman Eve. The name Eve means Mother of all Living.

Although having fallen, Adam re-aligned her spiritually by giving her a life producing name. He elevated her from being called a woman to being called Mother Of All Living. He set into motion a precedent for women to bring forth life to all living substances. Adam made sure he named her before they left the presence of God. The presence of God was an assurance that what he swore in His presence would stand. This act was an eternal binding force which would be the covenant connecting man and women to God. And God said Eve would desire her husband. The desire was also God's binding force, which would be restoring the spiritual covenant connecting male and female. However, this also meant she now had to turn to Adam to meet part of her needs having turned away from God.

When banished from the garden, Eve put into motion the spoken word of God. The desire for her husband kindled, and when Adam approached her, he knew her as his wife. The seed infused into her womb was life. There was an immediate activation of God's spoken word (Rhema), and she conceived and brought forth the first living being out of her womb. And Adam's spoken word as well, Mother of all living, the life-giving seed in the womb of women was released. (This became the first act of consummation binding man and woman together in the presence of God. However, this also set the benchmark for women's desires to be for their own husbands and husbands to love their own wives. Hence marital vows and all other vows as commanded by God between male and female are not meant to be taken lightly nor easily disbanded.)

The seed affirms that the purpose, vision, dream of God's for women is deposited first into her womb. The seed is symbolic of the purpose, vision, dream she carries full term, or she aborts before maturity. At full term, she does not relinquish her seed, i.e., the vision, purpose, dream, or goal, regardless of the length of time. Aborting is relinquishing it because of the challenges encountered along the journey of life. However, through perseverance, if persistent at some stage, delivery of the life-giving, God-given purpose, vision, or dream will manifest.

Adam, having disobeyed God and eaten what had come from the ground, had to now look to the ground for nourishment for his sustenance, and upon his death, return to dust. However, God did not take his male wholeness away from him. His spiritual connection and communion with God was his ability to produce life through the consummation with Eve. To Eve He said she would conceive and in pain, she would surely bring forth children. Although she would conceive in pain, naming Eve Mother of all living Adam took away any curse that would have befallen her. He annulled the curse from bringing forth any dead matter. He reiterated God's heart desire for the elevation of wives by their husbands. Pronouncing blessings over them would ensure they gave life to their homes, children, businesses, communities, and nations, etc.

When God said husbands were to love their wives, He concluded that she would also be a fruit-bearing helpmate in a union. In a union, a husband is not to curse or speak negatively over his wife as this destroys the life-giving seed within her. In blessing her, he blesses himself. Blessings are on the home, business, community, and nation, etc., as well. So whatever they would bring forth together, would live (be blessed). Regardless of the status of a woman, the fruit-bearing seed she carries in her womb never dies. Read Acts 9:36-42

2

ACHSAH

ADORNED – BURST THE VEIL

From the book of Joshua 15:16-19, we extract the story of Caleb's daughter, Achsah. She has a double-barrel meaning to her name, Adorned, and Burst-The Veil. She will be the next leading lady we explore. In this narrative, we unpack three benedictions in the name Achsah bestowed upon women.

- God's glory and beauty upon the earth manifest through the creation of nature and women,

- Women's inherent ability to venture into the spiritual realm,

- The innate desire deposited in a woman's womb to nurture and to give life to the land (humanity) through a God-given vision, purpose, dream.

ADORNED

'Adorned' expresses the visual presentation of God's glory and beauty in women that's manifest in the physical realm.

'Adorned' also endorses the hand of God's blessing of wisdom on the head of a woman, and the inner strength that He has embedded in her. The endorsement validates her right to adorn the glory and beauty of God, an understanding that women fearfully and wonderfully created in Him. Affirmation as the carrier of His glory and beauty, unleashes her potential and catapults her into untapped spiritual dimensions. When Adorned in His love and righteousness, she recognizes her self-worth in the way God perceives her, 'Carrier of His Glory and Beauty.'

In *Joshua 15:16, Caleb said, "He who attacks Kirjath Sepher and takes it, to him, I will give Achsah my daughter as wife."*

For Achsah, the first natural blessing was a father – an overseer/covering, a husband -protector/helpmate, the field - purpose/vision, and the lower and upper spring-provision/wisdom. These natural blessings were the manifestation of God's external adornment of His glory and beauty upon the earth through a woman.

'Adorned' also exhibits an external glory and beauty of the Lord's, displayed in His creation for humanity.

Jeremiah 31:4 'Again, I will build you, and you shall be rebuilt. O virgin of Israel. You shall again be adorned with your tambourines. And shall go forth in the dances of those who rejoice.

Having fallen, it is God who rebuilds, restores, purifies, covers with joy, sends forth, releasing a joy for all, which is an inherent characteristic of His Glory conveyed in and through women.

Honoring his pledge to Othniel, Caleb gave him the land he had promised and Achsah his daughter in marriage. After her marriage to Othniel, Achsah persuaded him of the need for a field of her own.

Joshua 15:18a Now it was so, when she came to him, that she persuaded him to ask her father for a field.

When she came to her husband, it was 'how' she 'came' to him. Being granted her request, we can infer it was intimately and in humility. This act enabled her to persuade him to ask her father to give her the field. Othniel was able to grant her her request. However, it was also to Caleb, her father, that she went for wisdom on how to sustain her blessings.

Joshua 15:18 So she dismounted from her donkey, and Caleb said to her, "What do you wish?" She answered, "Give me a blessing; since you have given me land in the South, give me also springs of water." So he gave her the upper springs and the lower springs.

The lower springs are indicative of the blessings from above poured out upon the earth below(lower). The earth reciprocates by yielding a fruitful land – a people obedient to the rule of the law of the land. The by-product of obedience is peace, brotherly love, economic prosperity, social prosperity, etc. that, through her vision, her purpose she can bring forth. Her field is productive and not barren, a land of fertile soil. For the land to remain fertile, productive, and prosperous, the right heart attitude is required. True motives for acquiring and asking for it in the first place are also a prerequisite. The heart contains living waters from which springs forth the issues and challenges of life.

Achsah persuaded Othniel, her husband, to ask her father for a field and then went directly to her father to ask for the springs of water for her field.

Achsah's act of approaching Othneil first is a form of respect, acknowledging his headship in the union. Approaching her father, he gave her the lower springs (that which is below, the field i.e. provision, family, community, nation, etc.), and the upper springs (that which is from above i.e. wisdom, understanding, knowledge and the fear of the Lord) on how to maintain the field, i.e. the vision, dream, purpose.

The upper springs were symbolic of the life-giving heavenly wisdom. They released the inherent nature of godly resources of understanding, kindness, gentleness, patience, love, joy, peace, longsuffering, self-control, faithfulness. In other words, she was saying since you have given me these natural blessings, these fields/land, a husband, a family, a community, a nation, i.e., material blessings, give me springs of water, spiritual blessings to maintain the natural blessings.

BURST THE VEIL

In the name 'Burst The Veil' we unpack a further three benedictions bestowed upon women;

- Insight into the Old and New Testament and the capability to excavate the rich treasures hidden in God's word.

- The revelation of secrets, in the Beginning, and the Central message. The unveiling of the End Times.

- The ability to spiritually amalgamate the Old and New Testaments. Ability to usher in the new dispensation in preparation for the End Times.

'Burst the Veil' has the intent and purpose of the rightful invasion of women into the spiritual realm. *The secret things belong to the Lord Deuteronomy 29:29, but those revealed belong to us and to our children forever,* and women can express these secrets in the natural realm.

'Burst the Veil' depicts the act of not just the outward removal of the veil covering the head, but more significantly, the veil that covers the spiritual eyes. The portal into the Holy of Holies burst open.

'Burst The Veil' is also symbolic of the pulling down of the veil that had been the partition between women and God. Achsah is the foreshadow symbolizing what took place when Jesus was on the cross. The tearing of the veil shattered and stripped away torturous afflictions, whether self-inflicted or placed upon women by humanity. Circumstances and some of life's appalling and unavoidable challenges that would inhibit the fulfillment of purpose and destiny were uprooted, overthrown, and destroyed.

The visualization of the stone that stood in the way of purpose, destiny, peace of mind, breakthrough, etc., must be seen as being rolled away.

Matthew 27:51 'Then, behold, the veil of the temple was torn in two from top to bottom;

And the visualization of the veil of the temple torn from top to bottom must be seen as pulling down strongholds from the top, i.e., from the crown of her head,-temple of God (thoughts, actions, etc. that which separates from Christ. Instead, infusing the mind of Christ,

Philippians 2:5 Let this mind be in you which was also in Christ Jesus – Isaiah 26:3 You will keep him in perfect peace, whose mind is stayed on You) to the bottom, i.e. soles of her feet and then shod with the preparation of the gospel of peace; (*Ephesians 6:15 and having shod your feet with the preparation of the gospel of peace*) to do the work of God prepared for you; (*Ephesians 2:10 For we are His workmanship, created in Christ Jesus for good works, which God prepared beforehand that we should walk in them*)

We are the temple of the living God. The veil that separated us has been torn, allowing us direct access into the heart of God, becoming one with Him in Spirit. But the most abominable and repugnant spirit against God's Spirit is gossip. Gossip is the obstinate spirit of an untamed tongue;

I Timothy 5:13. Besides, they are likely to become lazy and spend their time gossiping from house to house, getting into other people's business, and saying things they shouldn't.

Gossiping is an unrepentant heart and uncontrolled spirit. Gossip not only short-circuits a woman's purpose but is the obstacle to the actualization of her breakthrough to the promises of God that would enhance and catapult her to her destiny.

Hebrews 10:22 Let us go right into the presence of God with true hearts fully trusting Him.

1 Corinthians 3:16 Do you not know that you are the temple of God and that the Spirit of God dwells in you?

1 Corinthians 6:19 Or do you not know that your body is the temple of the Holy Spirit who is in you, whom you have from God, and you are not your own?'

When the veil tore in two

Matthew 27:54 So when the centurion and those with him, who were guarding Jesus, saw the earthquake and the things that had happened, they feared greatly, saying, 'Truly this was the Son of God!'

The men who were guarding Jesus saw; first, they then believed. The women who stayed with Jesus believed first and then saw.

John 19:25 Standing near the Cross were Jesus' Mother and His mother's sister, Mary, the wife of Clopas and Mary Magdalene (who had anointed Him, preparing Him for His burial Mark 14:8).

Achsah also laid the foundation for the art of skillful persuasion. Once Christ removed the veil, she lays a glorious foundation for the attainment of the glorious things of God. She removes the myth that women are inadequately equipped and not bold enough to ask God for the understanding and the decoding of the secret treasures of heaven hidden in His word.

Approaching God as Achsah approached her father opens the doorway for women to approach God boldly. He not only reveals His plan and purpose for them, but they can boldly ask for their blessings.

When approaching God, our Father, for the upper springs, it is also asking for wisdom through Jesus and wisdom is then imparted on how to execute and maintain the field/land, i.e., the vision, dream, goal, etc. We then utilize the blessing that He has given us in our various spheres or areas of influence.

In partnership with her husband, having obtained the field, she went directly to her father, and he asked what she wished and;

Joshua 15:18b-19 So she dismounted from her donkey, and Caleb said to her, "What do you wish?' She answered, "Give me a blessing since you have given me land in the South, give me also springs of water." And he gave her the upper springs and the lower springs.

Achsah removed the veil inherited from Eve because of her disobedience. This sin shaped mans' history and human nature and has perpetuated throughout the generations closing the spiritual eyes of humanity. However, Achsah gave women access to the presence of God. They could ask for their spiritual and natural inheritance. Once more, women's dependence was placed on God to meet their needs through Christ Jesus. This privilege disclosed divine revelation, its interpretation, prophetic words, words of knowledge, etc. It gave women the ability to tap into the heavenly vault and to pull out the treasures of heaven yet undisclosed in the word of God. It released their earthly inheritance of both the material and spiritual provision for the fulfillment of their purpose on earth.

As the veil tore in two in;

Matthew 27: 51 Then behold the veil of the temple was torn in two from top to bottom, and the earth quaked, and the rocks were split.

As the veil tore in two and Jesus took His last breath on the cross, it was a simultaneous release of His Spirit upon the women who stood watch over His body. His Spirit also allows women access to boldly enter into the throne room of grace at any time to receive help in times of refreshing and in times of need.

When Moses came down from the mountain, he covered his face with the veil to conceal the glory of God. To this day, in the reading of the Old Testament, some still have the veil over their eyes.

Exodus 34:33 And when Moses had finished speaking to them, he put a veil on his face.

2 Corinthians 3:13-14 'Unlike Moses, who put a veil over his face so that the children of Israel could not look steadily at the end of what was passing away, But their minds were blinded. For until this day, the same veil remains in the reading of the Old Testament because the veil is taken away in Christ. Read *2 Corinthians 3:1-18*

Today the same veil covers the spiritual eyes of many women. The inability to comprehend what Jesus did on the Cross speaks volumes. The profound meaning of Achsah's name signified boldness. It was the open gateway for women to enter and to access God's will for their lives. His will would be the significant role they were to play for humanity.

But Achsah's bursting of the veil has enabled women not only to understand the reading of the Old Testament but to excavate the rich treasures of God's word in its totality. These secrets are from the beginning (Father, Son, Holy Spirit), revealing the central message (Jesus the Messiah) and the close of the age(Coming of the Lord Jesus). These treasures afford women the grace to access the revelation of the old and to usher in the new things that God wants to do in this end time.

In *Joshua 15:16, Caleb said, " He who attacks Kirjath Sepher and takes it to him I will give Achsah my daughter as wife."*

The duty of a father, as commanded by Caleb, is to ensure his daughter given in marriage is to a responsible and capable man. For the man to receive his daughter's hand in marriage, he was to prove himself as a fierce warrior, spiritually, and mentally competent. Othniel's acceptance of the challenge was also an acknowledgment of what Achsah would be capable of producing and would bring into the union. His maturity and self-confidence enabled her to pursue God's calling for her life. Eve's name, 'Mother Of All Living,' was passed onto her generation. Whatever her field produced enabled her to give life to her family, community, nation, i.e., vision, goal, dream.

The responsibility for both men and women in a marital union or as single individuals is to produce good fruit in the field/land He has given them. Both men and women, therefore, have a choice to build up or pull down, i.e., self, families, friends, communities, or their nations.

Wise men and women build their house/land, but the foolish pulls it down with their hands.

Proverbs 14:1 The wise woman builds her house, but the foolish pulls it down with her hand.

The field/land (i.e., roles women are capable of fulfilling) given to women are sometimes in the hands of men. But because some do not have the upper springs (Godly wisdom) to sustain the land, it runs dry. They hold onto the land unyielding to give up the power, the status, and the riches of the land that feed and fuel the greed. What follows is destruction, corruption, poverty, unemployment, etc., upon the land. The manipulation of external forces continues to invade the lands. The lower springs are vulnerable/weaker lands. Heads of states compromise and bow to gods of greed and destruction, exposing their citizens to the wiles of the enemy.

In partnership with Christ, with the right heart attitude, women now have direct access to God the Father to ask for their field/land, i.e., communities, nations, ministries, businesses, families, etc. The gateway is their intimate and humble relational approach and persuasion through prayer, praise, worship, and fellowship, etc. Women can boldly ask, 'give me a blessing since you have given me this field/land – vision, goal, dream.' 'Give me springs of water, i.e., heavenly wisdom needed to bless the community/nation, raise the family, maintain the business, conduct the ministry, etc. which are the natural resources You have given me.'

V19b: 'So he gave the upper springs and the lower springs.'

Even women who have not borne children have a social responsibility to their (field/ land) communities/nations etc.

Isaiah 54:1-3 says, 1. Sing O barren, You who have not born! Break forth into singing, and cry aloud. You who have not labored with child! For more are the children of the desolate than the children of the married woman," says the Lord.

2. "Enlarge the place of your tent, And let them stretch out the curtains of your dwellings; Do not spare; Lengthen your cords, And strengthen your stakes.

3. For you shall expand to the right and to the left, And your descendants will inherit the nations, And make the desolate cities inhabited.

Biological birth is not a prerequisite for women to make desolate cities habitable, for God has spiritual children for her to embrace. Not only the birth of spiritual children, but the birth of a God purposed vision. The 'tent' signifies a dwelling, ministry, business, etc. Enlarge the tent signifying the enlargening of the heart so God can enlargen your 'tent,' your vision, field, ministry, etc. The possibilities of expanding and changing communities and nations through the birth of the descendants from spiritual children will make desolate communities, cities, and nations habitable once more.

3

MAHLAH, NOAH, HOGLAH, MILCAH, TIRZAH – DAUGHTERS OF ZELOPHEHAD

An acknowledged certainty is that God has given women the intuitive instinct of recognizing the hurts of the impoverished regardless of their social influence, status, or lack thereof. He has also endowed women with the sensitivity of feeling for the hurting world and the wisdom of addressing these inadequacies and injustices. Women are catalysts for effective change, and God has given them an innate skill and ability to herald and to manifest His goodness. Social problems that beset families and communities can and in the vast majority of cases be resolved by women as well.

Lack of knowledge of this truth, influenced by the environmental surroundings, lack of education, and various other limitations, e.g., marginalized social backgrounds, etc. may hinder or blind women to this truth. For positive change to be effective, there is a need for collaboration and networking among women. And a beneficial commitment to the relationship and partnership-building strategies. These are needed for women to uplift each other. For this to become a reality, women have to challenge the status quo, move beyond their cultural, ethnic, racial, and social status dissimilarities. They have to come to the understanding that they are spiritual sisters, born of the same heavenly Father. Positive capitalization is to be centered on each other's strengths and to find methods to support and empower each other. Each can bring meaningful discourse, practical, and workable concepts to the drawing table.

These recommendations can contribute to changes that will ultimately play a significant role in the uplifting of humanity, families, communities, cities, and nations. However, without resources, this cannot be possible. Looking to man to provide the resources, or for direction and destiny, is not only an impossible feat, but it can short-circuit the ultimate purpose and call in a woman's life.

The only One who can give women direction and destiny is God, the Creator. He can, however, use men or women to prophesy, confirm and edify towards attaining the God-ordained purpose. He is also the only one who gives visions, provides provision for the vision and the reservoirs to assist in the fulfillment of the vision. And again, He can impress upon whom He has chosen to assist in providing the different types of resources needed.

Every woman has an in-built creative talent or gift that is an inheritance to be claimed from God if yet unclaimed. The creative gift or talent can be a vision or call that is manifest in a business venture, ministry, in the political arena, academia, in Non-Profit Organisations, or Non-Government Organisations, etc. For far too long, women have been stifled, stymied, vilified by the myth that it's a man's world.

I believe the daughters of Zelophehad paved the way for women to receive their inheritance as God intended. The inheritance is to influence and to exercise their purpose in whatever sphere, corporately, or spiritually, God wants to use it in. The daughters of Zelophehad set a paradigm to be replicated by women to receive their inheritance, if not from biological fathers, then from God the Heavenly Father. It is necessary to bear in mind that the God-given purpose or vision is not for selfish ambition. The use of the purpose or vision is for the betterment of the lives of families, communities, cities, and nations.

In the Old Testament, women never received an inheritance; sons awarded preferential treatment. The inheritance passed onto the male figures of the family. According to the Israelite cultural tradition, the first blessing was bestowed upon the firstborn son and to those who followed.

But *Numbers 27: 1-7* says, *"Then came the daughters of Zelophehad, the son of Hepher, the son of Gilead, the son of Machir, the son of Manasseh, from the families of Manasseh, the son of Joseph; and these were the names of his daughters: Mahlah, Noah, Hoglah, Milcah, and Tirzah. And they stood before Moses, before Eleazar the priest, and before the leaders and all the congregation, by the doorway of the tabernacle of meeting, saying: "Our father died in the wilderness; but he was not in the company of those who gathered together against the Lord, in company with Korah, but he died in his own sin: and he had no sons. Why should the name of our father be removed from among his family because he had no sons? Give us a possession among our father's brothers. So Moses brought their case before the Lord. And the Lord spoke to Moses, saying, "The daughters of Zelophehad speak what is right; you shall surely give them a possession of an inheritance among their father's brothers, and cause the inheritance of their father to pass to them.*

The daughters of Zelophehad were not only bold enough to go before Moses and Eleazar the priest but went before the entire congregation. They also said they wouldn't bear the sin of their father. They wanted their portion of the inheritance. God said to Moses what they spoke was right.

They set the standard for women to be bold. Women could now come boldly before the throne room of grace. They could ask, "what is my purpose in the kingdom of God?" "Where is my portion of the inheritance? It has to manifest to leave a significant mark in the wellbeing of humanity on the earth?" They eliminated the fear of man. The demand for their inheritance was also for their father's name to remain among his family.

This speaks of women taking their stand to fight against the issues that try to obliterate the Name of the Lord in institutions, in homes, schools, communities, etc. Men and women in prominent positions have failed to defend the name of the Lord. The daughters of God must arise and refuse the annihilation of the Father's Name because those occupying seats of authority have refrained from upholding His name.

The daughters of Zelophehad went directly to Moses to ask for their inheritance. Moses is the foreshadow of the Saviour. He paved the way for us to go directly into the throne room of grace to our Heavenly Father. Here we can ask for our inheritance where Christ the forerunner has entered for us.

Hebrew 10;19 says, "Therefore, brethren having the boldness to enter the Holiest by the blood of Jesus, a new and living way which He consecrated for us, through the veil, that is, His flesh.

They also refused to bear their father's sin. Neither did they allow anything to stand in their way of receiving their inheritance. No generational curses, toxic negative genetic inheritance, no destructive past baggage, should block your inheritance. Geographical locations, environmental circumstances, or discriminatory elements should not stand in the way of receiving your inheritance. God has promised;

Hebrew 10; 16-17 This is the covenant that I will make with them after those days says the Lord; I will put My laws into their hearts, I will write them in their minds, then He adds, their sins and their lawless deeds I will remember them no more.

Like Achsah, in Joshua 15:16-19 and in Numbers 27:1-11, we find the daughters of Zelophehad followed suit and boldly approached Moses and Eleazer, the priest, with a similar request. They asked for their inheritance, which was their land. The land would have been their father's portion had he lived and entered the promised land. They, too, set a precedent for the generations to follow.

Seven years later, after Moses had died, Joshua and his leadership settled their claim – (seven signifying the year of completion). The delay does not limit the time frame in which to claim your inheritance from God.

Their claim is granted seven years later after being justified by God. During the seven years, we can only speculate on how they lived. Whether they lived beyond their means, a mediocre life, or an unproductive lifestyle, we can only surmise. During this period, was it within their capacity to accomplish their purposes? On the given time scale were their lives compromised until they realized that they had an unclaimed inheritance? But how they lived before receiving their inheritance is irrelevant. What is worth noting is the fact that they were able to inherit what was rightfully theirs.

The duration between the submission of the claim and its actual awarding is inconsequential. What is important is the hope and belief that God's promises do come to pass. God is not limited to a time frame in which to allow a purpose to come to fruition. The birth of Isaac came after Sarah had waited twenty-five years. Caleb's inheritance for his land materialized after forty years. The Lord Jesus performed His first miracle after thirty years. The list is endless of biblical patriarchs who waited a long time before receiving their inheritance or fulfilling their calling.

Hence the lack of resources, and in spite of the declining years, geographical disposition, or the time frame, should not be the primary barriers prohibiting women in fulfilling God's call upon the earth for His kingdom.

4

DEBORAH

OUR WARRIOR LEADER

JUDGES 4 AND 5

Our heroines in the Book of Judges are Deborah and Jael.

Deborah and Jael masterfully unraveled military-civil unrest that fashioned a pivotal turning point in the history of ancient Israel. The people paralyzed by hopelessness and fear as the oppression of a ruthless king abounds compelled Deborah and Jael to act on their behalf. This act ultimately leads to victory, and the glory snatched from the hands of men who yielded enormous power and placed into the hands of women. However, their God-given mission ends up in a blood-spattered war.

Deborah brought a nation to life and opened the political door to governance for her nation. She set a biblical precedent that women are warriors could, and can still rule and judge, making the world a better place.

Jael showed that women possessed the inner strength and unflagging courage to make brave, nation-life changing decisions.

DEBORAH – JUDGE, PROPHETESS; MOTHER IN ISRAEL

Undeterred Deborah, in her season, obeyed the call of God for her life. When Ehud died after subduing Israel's enemy, they had peace for eighty years. However, like the generations before, they too forgot about God's goodness and began to do evil in the sight of the Lord.

In Judges 4:2, we read that for the next twenty years, God raised a Canaanite king Jabin to oppress the Israelites. Hope was that they would once again open their eyes, turn from their wicked ways, and remember that they needed Him in all things. When they cried out to the Lord for help, He raised up Deborah, a prophetess, a warrior, a wife, and a judge to judge them.

The evil that prevailed in her day is no different from the evil that prevails today. Unique in her own right, she courageously dispensed justice while seated beneath a palm tree.

In obedience as directed by God, she assembled an army but had trouble persuading some of the tribes to contribute men to her general Barak's army. But her faith and audacity in the battlefield overrode their cynicism, and they won a decisive victory near Mount Tabor.

We journey together as we explore another phenomenal biblical figure, the story of Deborah:

Sitting under the palm tree, Deborah looked at the late sun setting over the distant horizon. She rose, picked up her bench, and entered her makeshift tent. There weren't many people on the road at that time of day as dusk fell, and the evening steadily approached. No one was likely to come, so Deborah decided to pack up, call it a day and go home. Besides, she was tired. There were hardly any cases to judge; lately, Deborah mused. Most of the complaints from the people were of king Jabin's harsh oppression that was tiring her. She set the bench against the canvas and was about to walk out when suddenly the silhouette of a female figure with her head and face veiled appeared in the entrance.

Jael had waited behind a cluster of trees until she was sure everybody had gone, and Deborah was alone. She emerged from the shadows and walked straight up to the tent's entrance. Crossing the threshold, she stood a couple of feet from Deborah and unveiled her face. Aside from being struck by her beauty, Deborah immediately saw the signs of stress etched across her furrowed forehead and the deep worry in her eyes.

"I am Jael," the woman said, introducing herself.

It didn't take Deborah long to compose herself after her initial surprise at the woman's bold entry into her tent.

"I know who you are, and I know why you here," she said, gripping Jael's outstretched hand.

Jael was momentarily stunned. "How can you possibly know who I am and why I've come to see you?"

"Your presence is the Lord's way of confirming His word for what He has asked me to do."

Shock and surprise replaced the worry in Jael's eyes. She immediately wanted to know how Deborah knew who she was, and the reason she had come to see her.

"Here, please sit down," said Deborah offering her a bench. It was obvious to Deborah that the woman was not comfortable being in her tent.

"Come, sit and let me explain the mysteries, workings, and wonderments of the God of the Israelites and His people," said Deborah putting her at ease. "Seeing you stand in my doorway this evening has not only confirmed God's message but has brought the greatest relief of my life. Our God has heard your prayers and trusts you to commission you with this deed."

Jael had no idea how to respond except sit and listen in mute astonishment as Deborah narrated the Israelites' journey with their God.

"What happens now?" Jael asked, sensing Deborah was through with relating her story.

"The wheels are already in motion, so don't worry, our God will protect you and your family."

Jael fell silent, feeling the weight of Deborah's message as it began to settle on her. She felt overwhelmed knowing she was part of their God's plan to bring deliverance for the Israelites, but not knowing exactly how.

The women spoke for a while longer before they both finally stood up to leave. They embraced, and Deborah pronounced a blessing over Jael before she walked out of the tent.

"Now, be careful, and remember the Lord is with you; you will be safe," said Deborah just before Jael reached the exit.

She nodded, threw the veil over her head covering her face, walked out, and was soon dissolved by the night shadows as she hastily made her way back home. The new moon was already rising above, and she was grateful for the light it gave, lighting up the narrow pathway. And back home, she was troubled by Deborah's warning and her strange request. 'Be careful, but do not worry for the Lord is with you. Make sure there is no one in your tent for the next couple of days, and you are to stay there by yourself.' But she felt she could trust the woman of God for no one had ever told her about her past, her present circumstances, and her future. How do you know so many things about me and the requests I've made to your God for my people?" she had asked perplexed.

"I don't," Deborah had replied honestly. "The Lord reveals them to me."

Jael had been even more curious about the God of Israel. She swore to get to know Him once the pending trouble weighing on everyone was over, she told herself.

She had no problem staying by herself as she pondered on Deborah's request. She was not afraid of being alone, but her heart pounded as she reflected on the events of the night. She felt an aroused sense of anticipation as she mused on their conversation. The trouble was what was she to say to her husband Heber to make him leave. She had to think of something and very fast.

The next day after Jael's visit, the day dawned grey and bleak. It was as though the weather, too, could sense the impending battle. Deborah took her place under the palm tree that stood between Ramah and Bethel in the mountains of Ephraim. The strategic positioning of the palm tree and where she had pitched her tent made traveling easier for all parties who came to her for judgment. Her husband, Lapidoth, had made the small tent for her to keep out the harsh weather elements. Harsh weather conditions would make her work difficult when she couldn't sit under the palm tree. Thank goodness for the tent, she thought as the clouds veiled the light and the wind came down furiously. She picked up her bench and walked briskly into the shelter of the tent.

The day Lapidoth had pitched the tent for her, had been an unusual morning. He had accompanied her early that morning up to the palm tree. Walking along the pathway, he noticed some altars that Deborah had ordered to be broken down. Debris from the goddess's altar lay scattered on the ground, and nobody had bothered to pick it up. The day the goddess' head had fallen to the ground, the sound had amplified the surrounding silence. The earth had trembled and shaken beneath Deborah's feet and those of her prayer warrior team. Their eyes had filled with foreboding.

"Oh my goodness," one exclaimed in fright. "Is the goddess angry?" she asked.

"Oh no," Deborah assured her. "It's Jehovah rejoicing to our first act of obedience. He said, "tear down all their altars in the high places, they are an abomination to Me and a snare to my people."

The women fell silent as they pondered on Deborah's words.

The majority of the scattered farms were throughout the countryside. Walking along the pathway, they greeted farmers who were close enough to hear their conversation. Some were already at work, pruning their grapevines. Shepherds were shepherding their flocks towards the fields, warm-jacketed farmers were milking their cows, and young children were collecting freshly laid eggs. The community was abuzz with activity before the expected threatening storm broke out.

But uppermost on Deborah's mind was Jabin's harsh oppression of her people. His ferocity and avidity for power increased. The incessant conflict and strife between them were getting worse. He continued to raid their camps and mercilessly destroy their homes, farms, and vineyards with his formidable force and iron chariots. Not only did he commit the most wicked and atrocious acts, but he also provoked the most unappeasable hatred among the people. On top of this burden, she had to contend with some of her leaders who viewed her as only a woman. And among them were the leaders of the city of Meroz, within the plains of Galilee.

"Now, Lord, You are asking me to tell Barak to go against Sisera, the commander of Jabin's army. Lord, I will not go unless You go with me," Deborah cried out on bended knees. She tugged at the veil over her head more tightly, as she prayed fervently. Deborah, engrossed in her prayer, did not notice the women who had accompanied her leave. Only her husband, Lapidoth, remained behind. He knelt beside her and prayed. After a while, he stood up. He lay his hand on Deborah's head, blessed her, and he too departed.

"I will go with you, just as I was with Moses and Joshua, I will be with you also. I will never leave you nor forsake you. Be strong and courageous" was the still small voice of the Lord. Deborah rose not only from her knees but against the oppression of her people. Their sense of purpose diminished as they were left powerless and helpless.

And Deborah Arose.

Judges 5:7 Village life ceased, it ceased in Israel, until I, Deborah arose. Arose a mother in Israel.

Judges 4:6a Then she sent and called for Barak the son of Abinoam from Kedesh in Naphtali, and said to him, "Has not the Lord God of Israel commanded, 'Go and deploy troops at Mount Tabor...'

Barak, known for his bravery and valor, came to her in his gleaming armor adorned with its trappings and ornaments awarded for his gallantry. The great warrior rode his horse around her makeshift tent and dismounted. He cast off his weapons, gave them to his armor-bearer, and came to sit on the bench beside her.

Barak was a powerful soldier accustomed to risking it all, but he had no interest in politics. He was tall, 6.5ft, slender, and agile. His features were strong and masculine, with dark hair and eyes just as dark. They were so piercing it was as though they could see into one's soul.

In the last battle, he had sustained serious wounds. He had fought unflaggingly despite the blood gushing out of his gaping wounds. He seemed to be supercharged by an unseen force as he barked out orders to his battalion who were spurred on by his courage. Even with a second serious wound sustained in close combat, he refused to give up until the enemy retreated. The day ended in victory, and he was finally hauled off to safety by his men.

He endured a long convalescence, and when he had fully recovered, he returned to his position in the ranks. He was indestructible, and he had just proved that he was a man who didn't know the meaning of fear. In that last battle the military skills, he was noted for had come into play. Injured and bleeding profusely, he would rather have died than pull back or show signs of weakening to his men. He knew they would not have regrouped and launched a counter-attack if he had recoiled. He also sensed had he withdrawn; his men would have panicked. They would have abandoned their combat position, and they would've lost the battle.

Now, as he sat across from her, Deborah could tell something was troubling him. "Are you not feeling well, commander?"

"No," replied Barak. He paused and then continued.

"You do realize we are advancing against a strong force; nine hundred chariots of iron and a great army that is with him. It will involve advancing from a great distance, through the desert, over the mountain, and across the River Kishon unless they cross over."

Deborah had responded unshaken and unabashed. "I know, and we shall advance."

Although encouraged and with a new zeal, he couldn't refrain from reminiscing about the violence of the last battle. It had been the bloodiest and fiercest campaign, the worst he'd ever fought with so many lives lost. He had seen so much slaughter, lives destroyed on the battlefield. Couldn't a stop be put to all the bloodshed, he pondered? For a moment, images of his childhood memories flashed through his mind. No fighting, the sound of laughter as he rough-and-tumbled with his brothers and friends. Was it possible to live in harmony, in brotherly love, to rise above hate and bitterness? Greed, the desire for power to control and manipulate each other, seemed to be the driving force that consumed the minds of men, he concluded.

The battle, his wounds, and the number of soldiers lost left him with visions that wrecked his mind. The memory of the horror of the bodies that lay strewn on the ground was so vivid, felt so tangible; he could touch them. When his men had for an instant almost abandoned their combat positions, he had felt cold sweat run down his spine. He knew had they given up; the enemy would have prevailed. If they had lost the battle, the enemy would have had no mercy for him and his detachment of brave soldiers. The only honorable thing in the event of a defeat would have been for him to end his own life. These flashes of memory had become more frequent. They attacked him with such ferocity and seemed so real that sometimes he could not distinguish them from the physical world or the supernatural.

"Barak," Deborah interrupted his morbid thoughts. A sudden feeling of acute sadness flooded through her soul. For a fleeting moment, she thought she recognized dismay and perhaps even remorse in the gaze of her invincible commander.

"A man of your rank should not allow regret or remorse to cloud his mind. We are not doing as our will demands but as thus saith the Lord. Jabin must be held accountable for harshly oppressing the children of Israel."

Judges 4:8 And Barak said to her, "If you will go with me, then I will go; but if you will not go with me, I will not go!"

Judges 4:9 So she said, "I will surely go with you; nevertheless there will be no glory for you in the journey you are taking, for the Lord will sell Sisera into the hand of a woman." Then Deborah arose and went with Barak to Kedesh.

Judges 5:24, *"Most blessed among women is Jael."*

The first time Jael had seen the soldier was while she had been stacking firewood behind the shed. When he entered the tent, she quickly tiptoed to the back and waited quietly in the shadows. She paused for a while to see if she had been seen or heard, and then began slowly inching her way around the shed towards the entrance.

She could not understand how her husband Heber had managed to keep peace with Jabin king of Canaan, who reigned in Hazor while he oppressed the Israelites. And now Heber was talking to one of Sisera's soldiers, commander of King Jabin's army. The man had come to Heber's tent just as dusk had fallen. He was alone and wore servant's clothing. Even though disguised, she recognized him as one of Sisera's men. The man had stopped a little way from the tent, had looked around as if making sure no one saw him or was following him. He had a sense of being followed. He couldn't shake the feeling that someone was watching him. From where Jael stood, she knew he couldn't see her.

As soon as the soldier entered the tent, she left her hiding place. She moved closer to the entrance without making a sound. She came close enough to be able to put her ear against the canvas. She wanted to hear what was said inside. The muffled voices and howling wind made it even more difficult to hear. All she heard was the faint murmur of voices. She decided a better position from which she could both hear and see would be on the other side of the entrance. She slowly inched her way closer to the other side.

She finally found a spot close enough to hear. But it was not too close that it would be obvious she was eavesdropping should she be caught. Jael lingered in the shadows at the entrance straining her ears to hear. After a while, she decided it was not close enough because she still could not hear what was being spoken. Heart pounding in her chest, she cautiously moved even closer. A sudden gust of wind picked up. She almost tripped on an unseen log lying on the ground.

"Ouch," she stifled a gasp. Quickly she lifted her hand, clasping it over her mouth.

Suddenly the man got up from the bench. "What was that?" he asked, standing up to go to the entrance.

Heber, facing the entrance, had just in time seen a fleeting shadow. He knew it was his wife, eavesdropping. He grabbed the man's sleeve. Delaying him, he gave his wife a chance to make her getaway.

"Wait. It's nothing, just the wind," said Heber, pulling him back onto the bench. "So, what's your mission? Why have you come to me?" he asked, quickly trying to distract him.

"Where is your wife?" the soldier asked instead.

"Visiting her family," Heber lied.

The lie seemed to settle him.

"We need information on Barak's strategic plan of attack. The deployment of his troops and the definite route he'll be launching his attack from."

"Wait, before you go, who sent you here and who are you working for?" Heber asked.

The man hesitated for a moment before he answered him. Heber had already recognized him as Sisera's soldier even though he had disguised himself in servants' clothes.

"Sisera," he replied. "My instructions are to provide him with advanced information regarding the route Barak and his expedition will take and the number of men he has recruited. We know he's preparing for battle against king Jabin."

As soon as the man left, Jael waited till he was out of sight and went rushing into the tent.

"What did he want?" she asked her husband.

"To know if Barak is preparing an attack against King Jabin."

"And what did you tell him?"

"Nothing, absolutely nothing?"

"But should his visit leak to Barak, who will believe you? You are the only house that enjoys King Jabin's peace," said Jael with a heavy sigh.

"You're right," Heber answered, a look of concern on his face.

"We must warn Barak immediately," she said.

27

"Wait, let's think this through before making a hasty decision." He raises his hands to his temples and begins to massage them. "Who do you think could be giving them this in information?"

"Could it be Kenesh, called the runner? He's on the fence, on both sides," said Jael.

"Now we don't want to be implicating anyone without evidence," Heber replied.

Arriving at her tent after her visit to Deborah, Jael was about to enter when she heard voices coming from inside. Immediately she recognized the soldier's voice. It was his second visit.

"What news do you have for me?" she heard him ask her husband.

"Nothing that I know of at the moment," replied Heber. This is dangerous work you are getting me into, and I want no part of it."

"Security costs, my friend, and peace comes with a price."

"Don't think you can threaten or intimidate me," said Heber harshly.

"I don't care what you think, just have the information I need next time."

"There won't be 'a next time,'" said Heber hotly.

"We'll see about that," the soldier threatened as he stormed out of the tent.

Judges 4:3 And the children of Israel cried out to the Lord; for Jabin had nine hundred chariots of iron and for twenty years, he had harshly oppressed the children of Israel.

Sisera was a violent man but also a valiant commander who had distinguished himself in the past victories he had accomplished for Jabin, the Canaanite king. As swift as a gazelle, he could run even on the roughest track and most hostile terrain, but this time exhausted by the battle, his strength would fail him. On both sides of the battlefields, the uncertainty of the pending battle unraveled the nerves

28

of the most valiant and bravest men in the history of Israel's wars. Both warriors Barak and Sisera had ill premonitions and grave misgivings about the upcoming battle. Barak was remorseful and exhausted by the loss of lives and the bloodshed. Sisera's confidence was failing because of the Israelites' recent victories.

And so it was that Jael also pondered on the history of her people. She wondered if the impending battle and her visit to Deborah would break the curse upon them. She had been praying for the removal of this curse. She wanted deliverance for her people from their idol worship of Baal. They had lived long enough among the Israelites, had observed their relationship with their God and she wanted the same relationship with Him for her people. He didn't demand the sacrifices that they had to offer to their gods. She acknowledged that her people were a snare to the Israelites and saw how it angered their God when they bowed down to her peoples' god, Baal Peor;

Numbers 25:1 for they harassed and seduced the Israelites with their schemes.

Reflecting on the actions of her people, she earnestly prayed for the curse that hung over them to be broken. She believed the prophetess's word that their God had heard her prayers and that He was with her. How did the prophetess know that she had been praying to the God of the Israelites? But then again, the Israelite prophets had a strangely personal relationship with their God, she thought curiously. Although a mite apprehensive at the strange request to be alone, at the same time, she had a weird feeling that something miraculous was going to happen.

The curse passed on from generation to generation was one that pursued her people relentlessly. She believed only the God of the Israelites could deliver them from the curse. She knew they were descendants of Cain, whom God had banished from His presence after he had killed his brother Abel. The story has been told repeatedly how Adam and Eve disobeyed God. Because the serpent deceived them, God cursed the serpent and said;

Genesis 3:14-15 "Because you have done this... I will put enmity between you and the woman, and between your seed and her seed...."

God had said He would put enmity between Satan and the woman and between his seed and her seed. Cain is said to be the seed that replicated the character of the serpent. Hence he was able to kill his brother Abel. He showed no remorse nor expressed any reverential fear for God by offering the alms he presented to God.

Genesis 4: 3,5,13-14 And in the process of time it came to pass that Cain brought an offering of the fruit of the ground to the Lord. But He did not respect Cain and his offering. And Cain said to the Lord, "My punishment is greater than I can bear! Surely You have driven me out this day from the face of the ground; I shall be a fugitive and a vagabond on the earth..."

The consequences of his actions were that God drove him from the face of the ground and out of the garden. God also hid His face from him. The entire clan had been nomadic ever since. They had lived among the Amalekites, and when King Saul was about to destroy them at one stage, he had instead spared them.

1 Samuel 15: 6. Then Saul said to the Kenites, "Go, depart, get down from among the Amalekites, lest I destroy you with them. For you showed kindness to all the children of Israel when they came out of Egypt..."

Because they had shown kindness to the Israelites when they left Egypt, king Saul had spared them. But now one of them was an informer. With all the information Sisera was receiving, it looked as though it was not enough. Now he wanted to solicit more information from her husband, Heber.

And when the Israelites moved from the City of Palms, the Kenites went and dwelt among them.

Judges 1:16. Now the children of the Kenite, Moses' father in law, went up from the City of Palms with the children of Judah into the wilderness of Judah, which lies South near Arad, and they went and dwelt among the people.

But her husband Heber had insisted they separate from their people.

30

Judges 4:11. Now Heber the Kenite, of the children of Hobab the father-in-law of Moses, had separated himself from the Kenites and pitched his tent near the terebinth tree at Zaanaim, which is beside Kedesh.

Was it perhaps what the God of the Israelites had foreseen and had allowed the separation to take place, for surely something phenomenal was about to happen. She pondered on her people's very existence and how everything affected their way of life as well.

The Kenites were coppersmiths and metalworkers. That year the yearly feast of the Lord's in Shiloh was about to take place.

Judges 21:19 Then they said, "In fact, there is a yearly feast of the Lord in Shiloh, which is north of Bethel, on the east side of the highway that goes up from Bethel to Shechem, and south of Lebonah."

Heber had made some copper artifacts for an Israelite customer. The feast was on the east side of the highway, and to deliver the goods would be a two-day journey. Jael thought quickly and decided she would use this excuse to get her husband to leave the tent. But there could be a delay if she did not help him to finish the order so she could send him on his way.

"Why the urgency?" Heber asked her as she proceeded to help him to complete the order.

"The feast begins in two days, and besides, we need the money soon. But most importantly, should the officer come back, I don't want him to find you here and to implicate you further in his schemes."

The soldier came a second time to their tent. He left his horse a discreet distance away from Heber's tent, loosely tied to a tree trunk. The horse had gotten loose and had wandered off. Returning from Heber and not seeing his horse, he feared it stolen. He put a couple of fingers in his mouth and whistled. He watched in relief as the horse came out from behind a clump of trees and trotted up to him. He quickly jumped on its back and galloped off at an untamed speed.

The soldier's horse raced down the road that twisted and unwound through the green meadows at the foot of the mountain. The fog had evaporated just a little. But he could tell the clearing wouldn't last as the weak moonlight reflected off the snow-capped mountain peaks. He doubled his speed, knowing it wasn't going to be a clear day ahead when daylight broke. He rode the whole night. He was aware of the need to change his horse that was showing signs of fatigue. But he feared to stop, knowing time was of the utmost importance. Having gathered the crucial piece of information from another source, he believed and depended on its accuracy and reliability.

Getting to Sisera was urgent, a matter of winning or losing the imminent battle. He snapped the end of the reins and dug his boot against the horse's flanks and urged it forward, pushing it to its limit. Finally, just before the sun rose, he saw a remote, low thatched-roof building come into view. He slowed the horse and approached the house cautiously. A dog began to bark and ran towards him. "Oh no," he thought, "he's going to give me away." As the dog got closer, it stopped and began to growl. He reached into his backpack, pulled out a piece of salted meat, and tossed it over to the dog who swallowed it in one gulp. The dog came closer, wagging his tail, looking for more. The soldier reached out towards him and began to rub his back and neck. This time he gave him a bigger piece. The dog sat at his feet like a long lost friend and began to eat his treat.

The soldier proceeded to the back of the house, knowing his newfound friend wouldn't let him down, wasn't about to give him away. The house surrounded by trees had a little stream running behind it. Further down the backyard as the soldier's eyes adjusted to the outside surroundings, he saw a couple of horses grazing close to the stream. He took his horse close by to quench its thirst, took his saddle off and put it on the back of the horse he perceived to be the strongest. He took off, leaving his mount behind. Fair swap, he thought, as he disappeared into the night.

The soldier rode mostly under cover of the night shadows keeping close to the woods along the road. The tale-tell signs of the brewing storm he had feared were beginning to show more intensely. Now and again, flashes of lightning lit his path, and still, the rain had not come. Not only was he racing against time, but against the foul storm that he could see was ready to erupt.

After hours of non-stop riding, he became less anxious, knowing he only had a few more hours before he reached the camp. An unexpected sharp bend on the road followed by a bolt of lightning, and the crackling of thunder spooked the horse, causing it to buck. It sent the rider headfirst into the trunk of an oak tree, snapping his neck on impact. He never reached Sisera.

Two days after Jael's visit to Deborah's tent and Heber's departure, Keshen the runner, entered Sisera's camp. He delivered the report that Sisera had been anxiously waiting for;

Judges 4:12-13 And he reported to Sisera that Barak the son of Abinoam had gone up to Mount Tabor. So Sisera gathered together all his chariots, nine hundred chariots of iron, and all the people who were with him, from Harosheth Hagoyim to the River Kishon.

Keshen, the runner, arrived out of breath, his eyes wide reflecting his fright. The intense lightning and the thunder were so ferocious; it was something he had never seen before. The angry wind had almost blown him off his feet as it blasted, tearing away at anything in its path. Was this a bad omen, he wondered. Perhaps this should be his last run as he contemplated the risks he had taken. In the past, he had no qualms about the information he sold and to whom as long as the price was right. He had never given a second thought to principle or political alliance. But now he had to reconsider. Now he had to contend not only with making people miserable but with the elements of bad weather as well. Another more serious issue was although he enjoyed the peace because of Jabin king of Canaan, he knew it was at the cost of the Israelites' oppression. He made up his mind that it would be his last contract. It was also about time he terminated his involvement in the dangerous line of work. Not only was it getting too dangerous, but the distances to cover were far too long;

Judges 4:12 'And he reported to Sisera that Barak son of Abinoam had gone up to Mount Habor.' And simultaneously;

Judges 4:14 Then Deborah said to Barak, "Up! For this is the day in which the Lord has delivered Sisera into your hand. Has not the Lord gone out before you?" So Barak went down from Mount Tabor with ten thousand men following him.

Deborah, Barak and his army got to the River Kishon just as Sisera and his army began to advance. Because Barak's army comprised mainly of foot soldiers, they waited on the river's shore.

All of a sudden, without warning, the sky turned completely black, and a stiff icy cold wind began to blow viciously, blowing at a rapid speed of 200mph. It was so cold it chilled the flesh and got into the bones instantly. A well-defined formation of clouds began to wrap around on Sisera's side as he began to advance. It was as though the predicted storm that had been looming overhead suddenly erupted. But the amazing thing was that as Deborah, Barak, and his men looked up at the sky, a miracle happened right before their eyes. The thunderstorm was earth-shattering as the Lord went before them;

Judges 5:4b-5a, the earth trembled, and the heavens poured. The mountains gushed before the Lord,

Even the stars diverted their course and shielded their light from Sisera and his army.

"Advance," Sisera shouted. His soldiers poured into the river towards Barak's men. But their plunge into the river was with a cloud-burst of hail and thunder. Sleet and rain turned the Kishon into a raging torrent. The result was that they couldn't see their way as the river suddenly began to swell. The storm intensified and became destructive and deadly. It made landfalls causing catastrophic damage at the place where Sisera and his men were coming in from to attack Barak. Wading through the river, Sisera and half his men managed to cross over, but the rest of his men didn't make it. They were slammed back into the water by the strong wind and turbulent force of the water. In seconds the river flooded. Sisera watched in horror his men thrown off their horses. The banks broke. Soldiers' screams silenced by the howling winds and gushing water. Arms flailing wildly, the waters washed over them, and his soldiers drowned before his eyes.

Judges 5:21 The torrent of Kishon swept them away, that ancient, the torrent of Kishon.

Barak and his foot soldiers slew the soldiers who managed to cross the river.

Judges 4:15 And the Lord routed Sisera and all his chariots and all his army with the edge of the sword before Barak, and Sisera alighted from his chariot and fled away on foot.

Some of the soldiers who had managed to get across the river had not foreseen the wheels of the chariots sinking into the ground. The ground had turned into mud, making it difficult to drive as the iron chariots became mired, leaving the charioteers easy targets for Barak and his soldiers. Using their arrows, slings, and swords, they caused mayhem on the battlefield until the last soldier was down.

And so it was that the Lord, *Judges 4:7 deployed Sisera, the commander of Jabin's army, with his chariots and his multitude at the River Kishon. And I will deliver him into your hand. 4:15b and Sisera alighted from his chariot and fled away on foot.*

Judges 4: 9, the Lord will sell Sisera into the hand of a woman.

The storm was a premonition that something dreadful was going to happen that day. Jael awoke with an indefinable expectation. Suddenly she felt an uneasiness. She stood unmoving at the entrance of the tent and gazed at the heavy raindrops. They pelted down hard and furious. She didn't move even as the cold wind blew gusts of the rain towards her, and the lightning threatened to strike her down. Then slowly in a deliberate slow-motion pace, she moved forward. And there, as she stepped out of the tent, was Sisera running towards her.

Judges 4:17 However, Sisera had fled away on foot to the tent of Jael.

Calm and composed Jael stepped out (of her tent, comfort zone, business, ministry, etc.). She responded to the challenge to defend and transform her territory and went out to meet Sisera. She said;

Judges 4:18-22 "Turn aside, my lord, do not fear." And when he had turned aside with her into the tent, she covered him with a blanket.

Sisera's fate already decided was brought to an end, his final encounter with a woman, Jael.

Judges 4:23 So on that day God subdued Jabin king of Canaan in the presence of the children of Israel.

Her song of victory is heard by all of Israel that day as she sings praises to the Lord.

Judges 5:2-3 When leaders lead in Israel when people willingly offer themselves, Bless the Lord. "Hear, "O kings! Give ear O princes, I, even I, will sing to the Lord, I will sing praise to the Lord God of Israel."

Oppression ceased. The economy boomed. Traders and travelers were once again able to travel on the highways and byways. Villages came to life as inhabitants enjoyed the liberty of once more interacting, networking with each other, with neighbors, families, and friends in faraway places.

When Deborah, mother of the nation, arose, she did not forget to sing praise and thanks to the rulers of Israel who had stood with her. It was to those who understood what they had been called to accomplish, who had not abandoned their God-ordained purpose.

Regardless of where one's roots are, whether temporary or permanent, when it comes to fighting for your people, family, community, or nation, hands must be practically put to the plow.

Judges 5:14-15,18 From Ephraim were those whose roots were in Amalek. After you, Benjamin, with your peoples. From Machi, rulers came down. And from Zebulun those who bear the recruiters staff. And the princes of Issachar were with Deborah, As Issachar, so was Barak Sent into the valley under his command. Zebulun is a people who jeopardized their lives to the point of death, Naphtali also, on the heights of the battlefield.

But there were also those who, while she fought for her nation, went about their agendas. They put their interests first and went about conducting their businesses. They did not understand their upward calling to uplift their nations. Self-gratification superseded their obligations. But others with courage sacrificed and jeopardized their lives even to the point of death in saving their nations.

Judges 5:15b-17 Among the divisions of Reuben, there were great resolves of heart. Why did you stay among the sheepfolds? To hear the pipings for the flocks? The divisions of Reuben have great searchings of heart. Gilead stayed beyond the Jordan. And why did Dan remain on ships? Asher continued at the seashore and stayed by his inlets.

Distance, migration, slave trading, trafficking, and the lists are endless of the causes that separate people. But the greatest division or separation is resolve of heart.

God's word has never changed. However, some institutions and churches, etc. have become lukewarm, and leaders continue to compromise, *Revelations* 3:15-17,19b, and some societies remain insentient.

But in *Judges 5:2*

And suddenly, Barak and the soldiers who had accompanied her exploded in a shout of praise, glorifying the Lord. When leaders lead in Israel, when the people willingly offer themselves, Bless the Lord.

Leaders who have the best interest of the people at heart, inspire the people to give themselves willingly to the law of the land and it prospers.

Revelations 3:21 To him who overcomes I will grant to sit with Me on My throne as I also overcame and sit down with My Father on His throne.

Judges 5:2-3 "When leaders lead in Israel (insert the name of your nation) when people willingly offer themselves, Bless the Lord. "Hear, O kings! Give ear O princes, I, even I, will sing to the Lord, I will sing praise to the Lord God of Israel."

When appointees anointed by God to govern His people, take the lead, and act responsibly, the people give themselves willingly. They are willing to serve the appointed who does what is right, who is wise, understands, and has a discerning heart. There are seasons when state heads govern a land inappropriately, and therefore life ceases, no production, no prosperity, no infrastructure, no industrial development, etc. The governors cause the land to follow other gods who are gods of destruction. The foreign demigods bring war, poverty, unemployment, corruption, crime, coups, etc. and there is no peace. Not only do they compromise the nation's wealth, natural and human resources, but in ignorance and unknowingly, they bow down to the foreign gods of manipulation, the spirit of Jezebel.

CONTEMPORARY JAEL

Righteousness exalts a nation (families, communities, nations), but sin is a reproach. Proverbs 14:34

Communities, families, and nations encounter challenges and complexities that appear insurmountable. But in each household, community, and nation, are women who look beyond their limitations and shortcomings and push back against oppression. They earmark and identify the needs of their communities, families, and nations. They take skillfully integrated and decisive action. With their faith and courage, they articulate for the voiceless who can no longer defend themselves. In times of conflict and uncertainty, they motivate a resolute movement forward. They endeavor to ensure peace and stability maintained amid crises. For those who are perishing, they ensure social justice served. Dashed dreams revived and showed empathy. Hope extended to those who wonder and question the very underlying primary purpose of their existence. They encourage and restore self-esteem and dignity.

Unfortunately, in some communities, families, and nations, there exists neighbors and leaders, etc. whose actions only bring devastation. These destructive behaviors generally fall upon families, vulnerable women, and children, impoverished communities, and can impact the entire nation. Because of these undesirable behaviors of groups or individuals, for example, 'Keshen the runner' in Jael's community, the rest of the nation had to suffer the consequences of his selfish and irresponsible actions. But Jael did not hesitate to bring justice for the nation. She did not act according to the differentiation of 'her people,' the Kenites, and the Israelites. She aggressively brought and held those responsible accountable.

Neither were her resources to execute justice in abundance. Her tools comprised a tent, a blanket, milk, a hammer, and a tent peg. An understanding that most women have these resources. Firstly they have a blanket to cover the nakedness of their families, communities, and nations. The nakedness can be a husband's flaws, a weakness in a family, community, or nation. A woman's nurturing instinct is to protect her family, community, nation. As no family, community, nation is perfect the woman's desire to protect them can be pardoned. As long as these shortcomings do not negatively impact her, the lives of the other members of her family, or the lives of other people. Neither should these flaws be foolishly excused or tolerated. Instead, she girds herself with the strength of the Lord's. She plans her day's work, does tasks to enrich their lives, extends her hand to the poor, and reaches out to the needy. Read Proverbs 31:10-31

She does not bring shame or embarrassment to her family or community. She uses the blanket to keep her family and community warm against the harsh environmental elements. She covers them against the cold and cruel realities of society's tongue, i.e., jealousy, envy, gossip, etc.

Her tent (a business, ministry, charitable organization, etc.) shelters her household and community. It becomes a haven from the cruelty of oppressors like king Jabin, i.e., drug lords, gangsterism, violence, etc. She has milk to nourish her household. The water is for the community whose souls thirst for living water in a dry and thirsty land. She eradicates poverty, substance abuse, etc.

Jael went beyond the care for just her household; she freed the entire nation. In choosing between Sisera (the minority) who was destroying the Israelites (the majority), she made the right decision. She did not wait for government intervention.

Secondly, she recognized that the most vulnerable and equally dangerous psyche of human anatomy is the mind. If the enemy can invade an uncontrolled mind or a mind-set trapped or paralyzed by helplessness or hopelessness, he can manipulate or control it. She silenced Sisera by driving the tent peg into his temple. She drove the peg into the temple is symbolic of the unleashing of the evil force (fear) that had captured the people's minds rendering them helpless and hopeless. She drove the peg into his temple, also signified a predisposition that had people reduced to a state of fear and who could no longer exercise the right to think for themselves. There was an inability to perform free-will thinking to its fullest potential of productivity. Sisera terrorized their minds. Oppression rendered them incapacitated. The tent peg driven through his temple silenced the fear and set the captives free.

Today the tent peg in a woman's hand is her spiritual resources (prayer, praise, prophetic declarations over herself, family, communities, nations, etc.) Her material tools are whatever resources she has at her disposal. Above all else, she has the word of God as her greatest weapon.

For we wrestle/fight not against flesh and blood, but against principalities, against powers, against the rulers of the darkness of this age, against spiritual hosts of wickedness in the heavenly places. (and manifest on earth) Ephesians 6:12

Wisdom bestowed upon a woman can silence a torturous mind set on inflicting pain on God's children and one that exalts itself above the knowledge of God. Read Judges 9:53

5

NAOMI AND RUTH

ARISE – LIFE'S A JOURNEY WITH GOD

RUTH 1:6-22

The book of Ruth recounts the story of Naomi, who found herself in a precarious predicament. One minute she was in a position of abundance, and the next moment, she was in a place of lack. Having lost a husband and two sons, she finds herself in need of 'bread.'

1:6 Then she arose with her daughters-in-law that she might return from the country of Moab, for she had heard in the country of Moab that the Lord had visited His people by giving them bread.

Metaphorically Naomi's are women in the Body of Christ who have to arise and leave the country of Moab. The country Moab is a situation, a place, relationship, etc. that once held a sense of belonging or well-being but later turned out to be a stronghold, bondage, or calamity. Formerly perceived as a place of comfort, safety, or familiarity because of what it previously offered, becomes a place or state of distraction, destruction, or low self-esteem? A prolonged problematic condition can also become part of one's life's journey. Its longevity, or several other demeaning factors, can anesthetize one to its existence. The predicament can make it difficult to see it or acknowledge its reality. It can bring a feeling of shame or a denial of its presence. Or the belief that deliverance from the dilemma is not possible. It becomes a stumbling block to your freedom and destiny.

The discomfort is the 'Red Light,' a signal that it's time to leave the situation, the place of sluggishness, complacency, mediocrity, compromise, or any places of destruction to your self-worth or moral value.

Hearing that God has visited His people and has given them bread can be through direct revelation, His word or prophetic utterance. The giving of bread can also be through modern technology, a social media platform, or any other medium of communication God chooses. The uncertainty or troublesome situation can become unbearable that it compels you to take action. The discomfort revives your spiritual antennas enabling you to hear that the Lord has visited His people and has given them bread. God's visitation need not be a geographical re-location necessitating an uprooting. It can be a spiritual awakening, that is a visitation of the Holy Spirit. A national revival, or the awakening of nations and tribes to their true identities in Christ, the giving of Bread in this end-time move of God - Jesus the Bread of Life.

Through the fulfillment of purpose and visions, women in the Body of Christ may inadvertently or consciously be emulating women like Naomi and Ruth. These women have the inner strength and courage to bring about inexorable waves of change to their families, communities, and nations. Every born again woman who has come to the knowledge of her purpose or calling in life is a recipient of this gift from God. The gift deposited before being formed in her mother's womb (i.e., purpose, vision, or dream)

Jeremiah 1:5a Before I formed you in the womb I knew you

The by-product of this gift is that it is a fruit-bearing seed that God has deposited into a woman's womb. It becomes a 'light bulb' moment when it's conceived in her heart; she believes in it and is prepared to follow it through regardless of the cost. The fruit that she brings forth is the manifestation of the (son) she delivers, i.e., the fulfillment of purpose, vision. He becomes a solution for the home, community, city, or nation, a restorer and nourisher of broken walls, i.e., lives to be built.

In Naomi's narrative, we see God's plan unraveling in the different seasons and stages of her life. When a woman finds herself in an identical situation as Naomi, but still maintains an intimate relationship with God, it enables her to cooperate with Him in the advancement of His agenda for her.

Today, women's roles have changed in astronomical dimensions. However, many are content with their current status, while those who are discontent find themselves challenged and unproductive in their social standings. Nevertheless, an untold number's primary concern is improving the quality of life for their people. Their occupation is to pursue this objective, which can cover any aspect of their lives they wish to utilize. It can be spiritually, materially, financially, corporately, etc. or in the area of influence, they believe God has called them to walk in. Together with women who identify with Naomi's situation, or who are on a different trajectory, we'll accompany her as she journey's with God.

Part one of Naomi's journey;

Naomi's husband Elimelech, as head of the family, we assume must have initiated the family's move from the land of Bethlehem, Judah to the country of Moab. There he dwelt with his wife Naomi and their two sons, Mahlon and Chilion. However, like every strategic move of God, this relocation too was orchestrated by Him. God caused the famine because he had a plan to fulfill through this family.

Therefore, God can cause a natural famine, a drought, or a spiritual dryness in our lives. The dryness is to move us from one geographical location or spiritual level to the next to fulfill His purpose. Hence we are not to despise the place of drought or famine in our lives, especially if it's orchestrated by God regardless of the duration.

Another example is the relocation of Elijah found in the book of *1Kings 17*;

1Kings 17:7-16 And it happened after a while that the brook dried up because there had been no rain in the land. Then the word of the Lord came to him, saying. "Arise, go to Zarephath, which belongs to Sidon and dwell there. See, I have commanded a widow there to provide for you." So he went to Zarephath. And when he came to the gate of the city, indeed, a widow was there gathering sticks. And he called to her and said, "Please bring me a little water in a cup, that I may drink." And as she was going to get it, he called to her and said, "Please bring me a morsel of bread in your hand." So she said, "As the Lord your God lives, I do not have bread, only a handful of flour in a bin, and a little oil in a jar; and see, I am gathering a couple of sticks that I may go in and prepare it for myself and my son, that we may eat it and die." And Elijah said to her, "Do not fear, go and do as you have said, but make me a small cake from it first, and bring it to me, and afterward make some for yourself and your son. For thus says the Lord God of Israel, 'The bin of flour shall not be used up, nor shall the jar of oil run dry, until the day the Lord sends rain on the earth.' So she went away and did according to the word of Elijah, and she and he and her household ate for many days. The bin of flour was not used up, nor did the jar of oil run dry, according to the word of the Lord which He spoke to Elijah.

When the brook dried and the ravens stopped feeding Elijah, God did not send him to a land flowing with milk and honey. Instead, he's moved from one dry location to an even more distressing situation. God sent him to a widow who had little to offer, a handful of flour in a bin, and a little oil in a jar. Elijah harkened to the voice of God, and the widow listened to the voice of Elijah. God's plan for both parties fulfilled. She stepped out of the 'me, myself and son,' mode and became of service to someone else. Elijah said to her, "Do not fear." Fear had already gripped her like so many have been consumed and paralyzed in fear of depleting their resources should they share. She had already conditioned her mind to eat and die. Because of a lack of purpose, and resources, many contemporary women have already died a spiritual death. A life without purpose, a spiritually unfulfilled call of God's, is an empty life. Fulfillment of Ged's plan is when we listen to His voice and His word. The surety that it is God's voice you are hearing is an absolute requisite. Obeying the word is imperative. This is regardless of the choice of medium, personnel, or communication God employs, or where He sends you. The resources-meager or in abundance– material or spiritual –that He has given us to utilize as a blessing for others does not run dry.

And so Naomi found her former place of abundance had become a place of emptiness. She had no husband, no sons, just two daughters-in-law, having survived both her sons and her husband. Then she arose with her daughters-in-law. The verses do not inscribe murmurings or complaints on the loss of her husband and two sons, the loss of her home, her old age, nor of being reduced to nonentity. Losing loved ones regardless of the surrounding circumstances, or the loss of material possessions, etc. is part of life's journey. Undeniable is the fact that death is intrinsic to life. Therefore a time of grieving or sorrow is permissible but only for a certain period or within a time frame an individual needs. To move forward, we have to arise from the loses, challenges, or other inhibiting or traumatic experiences that define life. These may also be divinely directed detours that are part of the storms of life God allows to move us. The consequences if we are unable to arise are exposure to the adversary who walks about like a roaring lion, seeking whom he may devour. See *1Peter 5:8*. The adversary will use the situation by weighing us down, blindfolding and obscuring God's purpose for our lives

Vision, dreams, and purpose come in different shapes, sizes, and capacity levels. If the vision, purpose, or dream is small, it's still from God. However, even though small responsibility and ownership lie with the visionary. The vision, dream, purpose can only be accomplished by the holder. God's intervention as a Father is only required for guidance in the fulfillment of purpose as a biological father would. But regardless of whether huge or small, impossible, or impossible to accomplish, it's still from God. Nevertheless, God's divine collaboration and guidance are essential every step of the way to see it through to fruition. God is not limited to a time frame, as in Naomi's case. Fulfillment of the vision, purpose, or dream may be in the declining years. But God is faithful and says in;

Psalm 92:13-14 Those who are planted in the house of the Lord, shall flourish in the courts of our God. They shall still bear fruit in old age; They shall be fresh and flourishing.

We have to decree prophetic affirmations over every situation. The declaration must be in alignment and accordance with God's word incorporating your situation. Declarations can be as the following examples;

"I will arise to fulfill my dream, vision, goal, assignment, commission that has been lying dormant, stagnant, or unrealized. The declaration must embody a scripture reference, e.g.

Habakkuk 2:2, write the vision and make it plain on tablets that he may run who reads it.

I will arise from the place of fear, doubt, disbelief, complacency, compromise, and low self-esteem, and every negative situation-scripture reference;

Psalm 27:1 The Lord is my light and my salvation, whom shall I fear.

I will arise from the place of insignificance. I will arise from a place where I have been made to feel I cannot accomplish anything in life that is of worth or value, scripture reference;

Jeremiah 29:11 For I know the thoughts that I think toward you says the Lord, thoughts of peace and not of evil, to give you a future and a hope

I will arise from the place of financial restraints, relationships, and unhealthy family situations, scripture reference;

Proverbs 10:22, 13:20 The blessing of the Lord makes one rich, and He adds no sorrow with it. He who walks with the wise will be wise, But the companion of fools will be destroyed.

I will arise from destructive habits, guilt, unforgiveness, scripture reference;

2 Corinthians 2-7 ...you ought rather to forgive.

I will arise and will dissociate myself from friends and peers who negatively influence my life. I will arise from vexations that appear insurmountable, scripture reference;

2 Corinthians 6:14 Do not be unequally yoked together with unbelievers. For what fellowship has righteousness with lawlessness? And what communion has light with darkness?

The list is endless of the negative situations we need to arise from, and so is the word of God to overcome them. But this can only be accomplished by engaging in practical action, speaking and declaring life over an unfulfilled vision, purpose or dream, etc.

God also caused Naomi to arise from the place of bittersweet memories. Fulfillment of one's plans does not cause the arising. The decision to arise is trusting in God, the promise keeper. A belief that God will cause all things to work together for good to those who love and trust in Him. Having risen, you will know where you are going, where He has promised to take you. A realization of knowing there is a place covering every aspect of your life, geographically, physically, spiritually, mentally, and emotionally — a better place than the one you at currently. And when you arise, you do not arise alone – your spirit who is one with God, arises too.

Your rising may not be like Naomi's who arose with people, her two daughters-in-law. Yours may be the arising of a vision, your purpose, a dream, a job, a spouse, etc., or whatever the circumstances are initiating the need to arise. Naomi had two daughters-in-law's, the number two signifying a double portion of the outpouring of God's favor. An unreserved trust in God releases a double portion of everything, inclusive of support and witnesses. When trusting God a, double portion of blessings, the anointing, favor, etc., are inevitable.

The double portion of the support structure may only be for a season. We know that both daughters-in-law did not return to Bethlehem with Naomi. Something has to give way. You have to leave something behind that will hinder your way forward to where God is taking you. Leaving behind may include material possessions. A progressive arising may also mean leaving behind people who were close and dear to you for a season. Arising and leaving behind is also inclusive of people who may be a hindrance to your progression and attainment of your purpose.

When it was time for Ruth and Orpah to go their separate ways, Ruth clung to Naomi, but Orpah went back to her people and gods. Disappointment is an unavoidable and emotional life experience when releasing those who are or were once close and dear to you. It's a heart-wrenching ordeal when they have to depart and go in their own predestined direction. Having invested in something or someone it can be emotionally wrecking to let go or when they choose to leave you. Regret or bitterness should not be part of the equation when they have to leave.

Naomi acceded the matrimonial union of her son to Orpah. She gave part of herself because Orpah became her daughter. Gratitude should be an integral part of our DNA for whatever God gives us or whomever God uses to enrich our lives. We see, even though Orpah left, Ruth chose to stay with Naomi. Our biological or spiritual children may have to leave us after we have imparted and invested in their lives, but that is part of God's plan. Though you will receive a double portion of people who may influence or impact your life, it is wise to bear in mind that you only have one life to live. God will give you the one primary vision, purpose, dream, assignment, or commission that you have to fulfill. For a season, you may have a support structure, and for a while, you may have to walk alone, just you and your spiritual hosts (your angels and the Holy Spirit).

Part two of Naomi's life fulfilled.

Having left Moab and gone back to the land of Judah, we see God's plan continuing to unfold in Naomi's life. As part of the plan comes into effect, we witness her return to Jerusalem only with Ruth. Orpah chose to return to her people and her gods. She walked in the flesh, therefore, desired the things of the earth. She looked with the natural eye and went back to the gods she could touch, feel, and see. The effects of the flesh and the materialistic trappings of the earth are temporary and are of no eternal value. However, on the surface, they may appear valuable, genuine, and people may be loving and affectionate, but all these conditions are only for a season. The natural, tangible things of the world will seem more appealing and desirable but are temporary, and things of the spirit are eternal. Naomi's weeping endured for the night when Orpah chose her people and her gods. However, her joy came in the morning when Ruth chose her people and her God;

Psalm 30:5b *Weeping may endure for a night, But joy comes in the morning]*

Ruth 1:14 Then they lifted up their voices and wept again, and Orpah kissed her mother-in-law, but Ruth clung to her.

The expression of emotional behavior, such as weeping and the physical act such as kissing and hugging, is part of our 'make up' our human anatomy and physiology. Weeping and the raising of our voices as Orpah did are internal emotions of sadness etc. expressed outwardly.

'But Ruth clung to her,' an outward action expressing an internal emotion.

1:15 And Naomi said, "look, your sister-in-law has gone back to her people and to her gods return after your sister-in-law."

Orpah still had residues influenced by her culture even though she had been part of Naomi's household. She still belonged to a group of people who had a different god. But when 'born again' although there is a diversity of a multicultural assembly of people, we all belong to one culture, the Jesus culture. Naomi prompted Ruth to pursue the same relationship with her people as Orpah;

1:16 But Ruth said, 'Entreat me not to leave you or to turn back from following you

With Orpah, it was a flesh communion between her and Naomi, a sense of touch, a kiss, and a hug. But with Ruth, she clung onto Naomi, resisted separation, was reluctant to part from her and held onto her. In doing so there was a spiritual impartation from Naomi into Ruth because Ruth said;

1:16 entreat me not to leave you, (b) your people shall be my people and your God my God.

She asked earnestly, begged, and beseeched her with all the impassioned feelings of love within. She wanted to give back to Naomi what she had received from her, her son, her love, and the love of a mother. There was a reciprocal exchange in the embrace as Naomi imparted the spirit of her God that was her inherent right into Ruth. And Ruth was able to look and see with her spiritual eyes, Naomi's God. *1:16b-17 Your people shall be my people, and your God my God. Where you die I will die,*

Just as nature differs in climatical seasons, so do people vary in their resilience, and differ in their degrees of loyalty.

But whatever season or stage you find yourself in life, God will connect you with your Ruth. The person will be someone to collaborate with you in accomplishing the plans and purposes of God for humanity. You may say you don't have a Ruth, only an Orpah. Discern and call forth your Ruth and let your Oprah go.

1:21 I went out full, and the Lord has brought me back home empty,

Naomi did not return empty, even though at the time, she felt empty. Bitterness consumed her. Under this emotional turmoil, she was unable to discern Ruth's role in her life. Neither did she realize the seed Ruth was carrying nor cherish it. She took Ruth along based on her persistent request to follow her.

Returning to a 'motherland,' with an unfulfilled vision or dream, may feel like returning empty-handed. But God still has a purpose for you to fulfill. It may be a spiritual journey you have had with God. Or a geographical re-location or an external cultural experience etc. But whatever the reason for your return, it will be to fulfill another phase of His plan for your life.

Let us pray we discern, appreciate, and value the Ruths with whom God has partnered us. Their partnership is to propel the vision, purpose, or dream to the next level of God's plan through the connection. Ruth must also be willing to take instruction and to listen to what Naomi has to convey. We see a reciprocal exchange between the union as Ruth begins to take care of Naomi in *Ruth* Chapter 2 and 3 (Read).

Part three of God's plan for Naomi and Ruth fulfilled

Ruth 1:22 So Naomi returned, and Ruth the Moabitess, her daughter-in-law with her.

When Naomi and Ruth arrived in Bethlehem, they met a relative of Naomi's husband.

Ruth 2:1 There was a relative of Naomi's husband, a man of great wealth, of the family of Elimelech. His name was Boaz.

Ruth 4:13 So Boaz took Ruth, and she became his wife, and when he went in to her, the Lord gave her conception, and she bore a son.

Only when Boaz went into her did the Lord give her conception. She did not give herself conception, nor did man give her conception, a conscious awareness that everything we conceive in life is from God.

Ruth 4:16 Then Naomi took the child and laid him on her breast, and became a nurse to him.

Hearing and embracing the call of God in one's life and receiving the seed, one has to be in one accord with the Spirit of God. The Lord allows the seed (vision, purpose, dream) planted in the spirit, to be formulated in the heart and then birth in the natural. The seed germinates, and the carrier bears a son (i.e., vision, purpose, the dream comes to pass) who becomes a problem solver, solution provider, and burden bearer, in short, the light of the world.

Naomi - The older spiritually mature women will take what the young Ruth brings forth. The birth can be a vision, purpose, or dream still being conceived spiritually or already manifested in the natural. 'Naomi' lays it on her heart, works, and nurtures what 'Ruth' has brought forth.

Jesus, born of the Virgin Mary, was the Son of Man who, in the natural realm, opened Mary's womb. The spiritual implication of this act signifies the supernatural opening of the womb of women to give birth to a God-given purpose. The birthing is the fulfillment of God's call. Whether the firstborn is male or female, or it's a natural or spiritual birth is irrelevant. When 'born again,' Jesus opens spiritual wombs enabling women to conceive the plan God has for their lives and to give birth to His purpose. And as Jesus became the light for all men, when 'born again' and women fulfill their purpose, the woman's vision, purpose, or dream for humanity becomes the light for men.

6

THE WISDOM OF AGE

FAVOR WITH GOD

With each generation, even among the older folk, mistakes have been incurred. No generation is perfect. Many folks have exercised wisdom through the journey of life, while many have squandered it senselessly. But despite some of these insidious acts, the waste, or lack of exercise of God-given wisdom, each generation has been able to garner acceptance from the Lord. Unfortunately, many of the unwise continue to walk in folly, deceiving themselves. With grace, wise leadership directs the younger generation. However, on the other hand, expedient on the wise to this privilege is the older folk's ability to walk in the ways of the Lord.

Nonetheless, some ideas and values will seem outdated and old fashioned to the younger generation. But the wisdom, foresight, and maturity of the older generation have been invaluable. Widening the generational gap is the millennium's innovative ideas. The millennium generation has fresh, innovative ideas. They think outside the box, and of course, have an endless supply of energy. Their accessibility to updated technological material, their quick adaptation, and integration of this technology is to their advantage. They are also able to expeditiously grasp and embrace the trends of the ever-changing dynamics of the world systems. But the engrafted word of God does not change, has taken root, and has borne good fruit in the older generation.

The favor of God is manifest in them because they know the wisdom of God through His word. Having consumed the word over the years, they have become one with the word and have become doers of the word. Wisdom is witnessed on Abraham, an example of wisdom on an older person. Lot found himself in an unfavorable situation with Abraham. When they had to part company, Lot chose the better part of the field, what his eye could see. Abraham chose his relationship with God.

In Genesis 13: 9-10, "Is not the whole land before you?" Please separate from me, if you take the left, then I will go to the right; or if you go to the right, then I will go to the left." And Lot lifted his eyes and saw all the plain of the Jordan, that it was well watered everywhere (before the Lord destroyed Sodom and Gomorrah) like the garden of the Lord, like the land of Egypt as you go toward Zoar.

Abraham's faith and confidence in God permitted Lot to have the better field. He was not moved by the operations in the natural realm, what the eye could see. Instead, Abraham operated in the faith realm. He knew and believed in the unseen God, an advantage he had over Lot. Lot's inexperience, walking by sight, and not seeking the face of God first, resulted in the impulsive behavior. The consequences of his action got him into serious trouble.

Genesis 14:12 They also took Lot, Abram's brother's son who dwelt in Sodom, and his goods, and departed.

These impulsive actions may be the case with some of the younger generations, who don't have the patience to wait on God. More often than not, they act impulsively on what the eye sees. The older generation, on the other hand, through experience and faith, has endured. Having patience, they have waited on God and have developed a dependent and trusting relationship with Him.

This faith and trust principle also applied to Naomi and her two daughters-in-law. Naomi had a relationship with God even though she felt;

Ruth 1:13 the hand of the Lord had gone out against her,

Releasing the blessings of the Lord when sending Ruth and Orpah away was an indication that Naomi walked by faith and not by sight.

Ruth 1:8-9 The Lord deal kindly with you; The Lord grant that you may find rest.

She believed the Lord would bless them.

Like Lot, Orpah chose what her physical eye could see, and her hands could touch – her people and gods. But Ruth saw in Naomi, a relationship with a God she could not see with her physical eye, but saw with a spiritual eye and believed in her heart. The relationship, the desired trait Christians should aspire too.; a trait that can draw non-believers to God. Naomi, through faith, believed and knew that He existed. She had heard that He had visited His people, giving them bread. In faith and trusting the Lord, she believed she would be a partaker in receiving the bread. Without seeing it, she desired the bread in faith.

And she arose that she might return from the country of Moab for she had heard in the country of Moab, that God had visited His people. Even though she felt His hand had gone against her, she could still bless her daughters-in-law with the love of the Lord. The blessing, an inner conviction that Naomi possessed knowing that God existed, regardless of her loss. And Naomi guided Ruth without manipulation, a strength many women of this generation may or may not at a certain juncture of their lives possess.

7

THE QUEEN OF SHEBA

INTRODUCTION

Numerous classical historians, theologians, and scholars have documented, and some have negated to record the similarities between the Egyptian Pharaohs and the Biblical Israeli Patriarchs.

We begin our story of the Queen of Sheba from her grassroots level. Although captured from a fictional viewpoint, we cover the biblical account of Queen of Sheba' and her connection with the Israeli Patriarchs, namely king Solomon.

We also bridge the relationship gap between the two dynasties, that is the Ethiopian Queen called Makeda, and the Egyptian Queen called Bilqis. In the Ethiopian Chronicles, the Kebra Negast, which is a 14th-century account, about 700 years old, she is named Makeda. Many Ethiopian Christians have appraised it to be historically reliable in its content. In the Quran, a religious text regarded as an excellent work in classical Arabic literature; she is named Bilqis. For this narrative, we conclude the Egyptian Pharaoh's daughter, and the daughter of Shar Habil, the king of Yemen, is the same person. Because she was born in Yemen and spent her youth in Ethiopia when she became Queen, she had sovereignty over both kingdoms.

Princess Bilqis, upon her father's death, is crowned the Queen of Sheba of both dynasties, Egypt and Ethiopia. For the duration of our story, we will import the Bible message about the Queen. Some of the parts used for the story are believed to be reliable and trustworthy. They are verifiable records of the events and details of the romantic adventure between her and king Solomon. I hope that the story inspires and encourages the 21st-century women called by God. As we learn we glean some of the Queen's wisdom, strength, and courage. Her willingness to forsake self-concerns in the interest of her people is motivating.

However, not all the queens who ruled in the 10th century, up to the 16th and beyond, were good. There was a diversity of the good, the bad, the weak, and the courageous. Some ruled with power and authority. Some fought battles, won and lost wars, and some under the weight of opposition gave up their sovereignty.

Still, others endured the responsibility to rule with fierce tenacity and audacity. Those who were weak or ill-prepared found themselves failing and instead of ruling, were ruled. High expectations were demanded by those who were well-groomed for their roles. Many were involved in long family and religious feuds. Many more horrifically branded witches or traitors and burnt at the stakes. A great number dictated, too, and some manipulated to do the bidding of strong-willed men. Still many forced, some voluntarily became regents to their minor heirs. An untold number were pawns in the hands of men whose aim for rulership was solely for their ambitious power games. Out of sheer frustration, some abdicated while others escaping execution chose exile. Still many dethroned by armed military coups. Incalculable numbers betrayed by their troops who defected to the side of their rivals. Nevertheless, we learn and echo the bravery of women from ancient history.

In the 21st-century, we salute and normalize the brave acts of women as decision-makers in public life. I hope these stories from both eras inspire us to be the voice for the voiceless, to advocate, and to fight for the less fortunate. Hopefully, someday, they too will enjoy the full measure of liberty and will experience and embrace the benefits of human dignity.

EGYPT AND ETHIOPIA

Egypt and Ethiopia, in all her glory under the rule of the Queen of Sheba, has expanded her territories beyond her wildest dreams. But beneath her victories lies the malicious threat of vicious men intent in dividing her kingdoms. As nature takes its course, her ancestors and not even Sadik her heroic and faithful commander-in-chief can succeed in suspending the flow of events that begin to unfold. The mounting pressure of the inexorable and evolving plot against her kingdoms intensify. She awakens to the knowledge of the fragility of her kingdoms. If she does not act decisively and seize the opportunity to arise, she will fail her people. Unless she avails herself and makes the dangerous journey, there will be a kingdom break down. The journey for better or for worse will ultimately change the course, the history, and destiny of her kingdom.

PROLOGUE

PRINCESS BILQIS

"No, no," was the ear-piercing scream. It awoke Faridah in the adjoining chamber and heard by Amarna, the eunuch who had taken residence outside the young princess's chamber. Amarna had begun sleeping directly outside the princess's bedroom door since the nightmares began.

In a flash, Faridah was by her bedside. She found Bilqis sitting upright on her bed. Trembling and shaking her head from side to side, the princess wept uncontrollably. Hearing the scream, Amarna burst into the room, rushing to her bedside as well.

"It's alright," Faridah assured him. "She's had one of those nightmares again. Go back to sleep Amarna. I'll settle her.

Amarna reluctantly retreated. He flopped onto his rolled mat he slept on and was soon fast asleep.

Faridah stayed with the young princess with her arms wrapped around her. She cradled her head in her arms until her sobs subsided. "Is it the same dream?" she asked the princess gently.

Yes," Bilqis answered softly. "But why does it seem so real? Is it a warning, is God trying to tell me something?" she asked her maidservant with a quiver in her voice.

"What can He be telling you that brings you so much, terror?" The question was directed more to herself than to the princess. "But don't fear, my princess, I am here for you, and Amarna has been sleeping outside your door every night. Neither has Sadik left your side during the day since your father passed on. You will be well taken care of, I promise," she said, trying to calm and pacify the princess. Faridah held her in her arms until her breathing became normal again. She gently lowered her head upon the pillow, and soon, the princess was once again asleep. Faridah tiptoed back to her bed and abandoned herself to sleep as well. She was lulled by the titter-tat of the raindrops on the roof while trying to comprehend the princess's sudden nightmare attacks.

Then one night, despite all the precautions and all the safeguards put in place, her worst nightmare became a reality.

Suddenly Amarna burst into the room, clutching his bleeding abdomen followed by three masked men.

"Run, princess, run," he yelled. He tried valiantly to prevent the men from getting to her, but one of them grabbed him by the collar, and viciously threw him aside. It looked like he had taken his last breath as he collapsed onto the floor.

Faridah managed to get to the princess first. Thrusting herself on top of her, she tried to shield her body.

The princess jolted from her sleep is awakened by the commotion. 'It's happening,' the nightmare flashes briefly through her mind. It was as though she was watching a slow-motion drama scene unfold in her bedroom. 'Is this the reality of the nightmare I've been anticipating?' She watched Amarna's bloodied body fall in a heap and felt one of the men yank Faridah's body off her before she passed out.

PART ONE

THE QUEEN OF SHEBA

RULER OF KINGDOMS

Adonijah Solomon's step-brother threatens his accession to the throne just before the death of his father, King David. His mother, Bathsheba, had gone to the king to have Solomon anointed as king, while Nathan, the prophet, and the king's counselor, condemned Adonijah's coup. Bathsheba went to King David to anoint and crown her son Solomon as king. Sadik, king Agabos's chief advisor, had him anoint and crown his daughter Princess Bilqis as 'The Queen of Sheba.'

Lying on his bed, the frail king Agabos knew his end was fast approaching. Summoning his trusted advisor Sadik, he expressed his concern for his daughter to be crowned queen before he died. His second wife, Queen Hagathia, wanted her son Amenophis to be anointed and crowned king of Sheba instead.

Sadik was aware of the Queen's wishes to have her son enthroned as king. Watching the king's health deteriorate, he persuaded him to hasten the crowning before he died. The king's wish was to nominate Sadik in a royal capacity as well. Sadik had emphatically refused the king's proposal. Besides, he told the king he would have an internal war because he was not the king's next of kin nor his late wife's. In refusing to accept the appointment, he hoped the king did not view it as a defiant act. Although still young, the princess was strong, and he preferred the idea of being her protector and advisor until she became of age. The king had silently nodded as he listened to Sadik's proposal.

Without the knowledge of Queen Hagathia, Sadik had secretly conspired with the king's trusted noblemen, friends, and advisors to have the crowning ceremony. He ingeniously devised a scheme to remove the Queen and Amenophis from the palace. He arranges they summoned to one of her tribe's villages on the pretext that they are needed urgently. Midday, the fragile king is donned in his kingly robes.

On his throne, he sat and waited for the arrival of his daughter. Bilqis had also been secretly prepared, hastily dressed, and escorted to the king. The young princess walked into the hall, the epitome of beauty. Her demeanor and regalia were befitting her role as the Queen of Sheba. Like Solomon, she's quickly crowned Queen of Sheba

THE SOLOMONIC DYNASTY

King Solomon and The Queen of Sheba

The Queen of Sheba's visit to King Solomon has been told and re-told from century to century, conjured to captivate the imagination of each generation. To some, the story's narrated and embraced as a love story. But to many, it's an ingenious biblical story that has shown the strength of a woman who ruled with power and authority. She has passed this extraordinary quality to women from generation to generation, giving them the incentive that they too can rule in the capacity as called and ordained by God.

She came to Solomon as Bilqis-- daughter of the Creator of the Universe. As Makeda – she was a woman of fire, priestess and unifier of her kingdoms, Queen of Sheban. She came chanting and uttering spiritual prayers as she knelt before her God. When she left Israel, she felt even more conscious of her spiritual connection and awareness as the precious daughter of the Most High God.

The message conveys the truth that God is no respecter of persons. When you come to Him as you are He anoint you, elevates and raises the bar to your conscious awareness of your divinity. The divinity within enables you to carry out His pre-ordained assignment for your life. And the relationship is deepened, and your divinity as a daughter of the Most High God is awakened and realized.

THE PROCESS - BECOMING

As a young girl, Bilqis would slip into the palace hall and hide behind a pillar to listen to the political squabbles and debates. She would search the faces of the seated men until she found her father, seated at the head of the massive mahogany table. As customary, he remained silent until every argument and debate heard before he spoke. And as usual, all the high officials, advisors and nobles would turn expectant faces to hear what the king would say. She was in awe of the father she loved and adored so much. At night she would lie in bed wondering from where he got his wisdom and so much insight. She was intrigued by the stories that came alive in those palace throne rooms.

Then one day, she was discovered by her step-brother Amenophis. He thought by exposing her; she was sure to be punished. If not by her father who adored her, he was certain it would be by the officials who were sure to vote for her punishment. But lo and behold, to his grief and disappointment; instead, her father had hired a personal tutor and made sure she received an exemplary education. He insisted she followed a rigorous curriculum that taught her everything from art and science to classics and politics, preparing her to be an excellent queen consort. Soon she was proficient in all her subjects. What Amenophis had intended for bad was turned around to her advantage. She sucked in every lesson like a sponge. Favored, she had access to the court documents. She was allowed by the palace scribes to read whatever she wanted to read. The tutor made no effort to hide her brilliant mind or to show it off. Instead, he would further stimulate and provoke her young mind, championing her to excellence. When lonely or when she grieved for her mother, she found solace and refuge in her books.

The Battle To Dethrone Her Begins:

Bilqis was devastated by her mother's death, but exceedingly more by her father's. However, she did not allow herself the gratification of a long mourning period as she knew what awaited her. Plots to wrestle the throne from her had intensified. Since the failed kidnapping attempt before her crowning and the close death of Amarna, the palace security had doubled. The kidnappers were never apprehended, and Bilqis wondered who they were. Top on her list of suspects was her stepbrother Amenophis. But thus far, nothing could be found linking him to the attempted kidnapping. Her parents had always protected her. But now, how could her mother and father protect her from the powerful nobles who clustered around her throne-like ravenous wolves? "What does she know about ruling two kingdoms? She is but a child. Who is will be her trusted regent? She'll bring the kingdoms to ruin," they whispered maliciously. But they had not only underestimated Sadik, her father's trusted advisor, and personal bodyguard but Bilqis as well.

After her father's burial, the council gathered for the reading of her father's will. The executor was Medinet-Habu, the High Priest to whom the will was released.

The will's read. A burst of indignant protest rises from the seated noblemen and advisors. Not only has the king made Princess Bilquis his successor, but she is to rule and reign over both kingdoms, Egypt, and Ethiopia as the Great Queen of Sheban. It also states Sadik is to be her regent until she becomes of age in two years.

The shock and surprise on Sadik's face are evident as all turn to stare at him. 'I told the king not to do this.' Amenophis and Queen Hagathia glare at him. Amenophis is the first to openly contest the will, stating that an outsider could never be a regent.

"It should be Queen Hagathia, she's the current reigning queen," he yelled.

"May I draw your attention to the invalidity of your argument. You cannot contest the will. Unless grounds for contesting are valid and yours are not. May I remind you that Sadik was the king's most trusted friend, warrior andadvisor. He is just as saddened and distressed by the death of a friend that he loved deeply and served with his life."

 By evening the matter is finally settled. Amenophis is the only one who storms out the hall, followed shortly by his mother and his supporters.

Without her father's will, Bilqis knew she would have languished into obscurity. She, without question, would be sent to her mother's homeland, and the throne taken away from her. But Sadik, anticipating their motives, knew that the familial threats were not just for the throne but threatened to destabilize both kingdoms. She could not and would not retreat.

Encouraged by Sadik's support, she proceeded to push her claim to the throne of the two kingdoms more fervently. Soon she began to excel not only in beauty but in the courage of a warrior king's daughter. She conducted herself with integrity and had the foresight of a much older woman. She brilliantly deflected marriage proposals from noblemen and young princes from the neighboring kingdoms. She wanted nothing and no-one to jeopardize her position in the kingdoms or the welfare of her people. She believed the union of the two kingdoms should benefit and reward both dynasties. She was maturing fast as she saw those who cast covetous eyes towards her rich in natural resources and fertile lands.

Under her reign and Sadik's supervision, the two kingdoms witnessed a rapid expansion of economic growth, trade, and infrastructure, as well as industrial and agricultural growth. Sadik impressed upon her to prove herself so that the people would believe in her leadership. The people would be on her side she would gain their trust and protection should there be another betrayal.

And so it is with the daughters of the Most High God who should be in awe of the wisdom and insight of their God. They no longer have to stand behind palace walls, or behind closed doors, nor in the outer courts. They can now stay in His Presence to find answers to the challenges that beset their purpose. These are answers obtainable through direct communication with God confirmed in the spirit and found between the pages of the life-giving manual – the Bible. The enemy (challenges of life) often thinks he has outdone the purpose of the daughters of the Most High when they are in desperate situations or walking outside the will of God. Trusting God, regardless of the dire circumstances, only magnifies and propels them towards God's will for their lives. God also reveals their purpose through the numerous tools He provides. The tools can be prophecies, word of knowledge, divine revelation, etc., and men and women assigned to work alongside them.

But unlike King Solomon, Bilqis hadn't cared for the throne. The only reason she had accepted it was to protect her people and to thwart her stepmother and stepbrother's greed.
They schemed to enrich their families and kinsmen through the gold, silver, the rich spices exported, and the tariffs they would gain. The other reason, should their plan have succeeded, was the division and

strife it would bring to the already fragmented tribes. She knew the Southern tribes would fight to retain their power if a Northerner ruled. Hostility was brewing, and the threat of tribal civil clashes was imminent. The only other person, the people, would trust to rule would be Sadik. But of course, that would have caused endless tribal conflicts. He had been the king's unofficial advisor and friend who remained in the king's service until he died. His gratitude to the king expressed in his service in the palace's royal army. He felt he owed the king his loyalty for rebuilding his life, erasing a purposeless life he had been locked in as a young man. Destiny for greatness was in his heart. An instinct of fearlessness and hard work earned him the promotion as the king's guard, advisor, and friend. The young Nubian lad had risen rapidly in rank. He became a brave warrior whose loyalty and concern for the king's wellbeing had surpassed all other warriors. The king's safety had been his priority. The crown was of no interest to him. His size in stature, his bravery, and his past victories as the king's defender had been to his advantage. Sadik was now transferring his loyalty and affections to the princess.

The Queen of Sheba had a defender. The women of God to have a defender, and He has given His daughters the Holy Spirit to be their guide and counselor. He has also assigned and despatched angels to encamp around them not only for their protection but to do the word of His bidding concerning their lives.

No sooner had Bilqis ascended to the throne when threats to divide the two kingdoms erupted. When Amenophis joined his mother, Queen Hagathia, at the royal palace, he ushered in endless conflict among the royal household. Men of different and conflicting loyalties began infiltrating the palace after his arrival. Intensifying the threat to the kingdom was the added burden of news received of king Solomon's agenda. The latest report delivered was his intention to cut short their Ethiopian and Egyptian trade routes by building a competing seaport. She had also received news of this great king's wisdom and his dynasties. After much contemplation, she decided to go and see for herself what she had heard from Manetho. Besides, she was curious to see his fame and the house he had built for his God.

She waited anxiously for Manetho the caravan merchant's return trips with bated breath. As soon as he returned, he would give the order for his caravans to be offloaded and to get his camels refreshed. Next, he would get himself cleaned and presentable to go before the Queen. He then delivered the king's letters. The letters always came with precious gifts of pure silk gowns, beautiful materials, jewelry, and anything the king knew befitted a Queen. The gifts, of course, aroused Bilqis's curiosity even further. She was emotionally stirred by his poetic letters of endearment and delighted by his gifts. Manetho's reports aroused her curiosity immensely. She was eager to see for herself his wisdom and the splendor of his kingdom.

The council and advisors agreed to let a delegate of their trusted members go to handle the negotiations. They were horrified when Bilqis said she would personally embark on the journey to negotiate the terms herself. She disregarded their warnings of the dangers she would encounter along the journey. But the other reason they did not want her to undertake the dangerous journey was the rumors of Israel's hostility between their tribes. They had heard of the friction and strife that ominously existed among the king's tribes. The North felt they were unfairly treated by the king who raised their taxes and levies and not the South's to whom he showed favoritism. 'Almost the same predicament my kingdom is undergoing,' Bilqis thought. 'Perhaps together we can draw from each other's wisdom and find a resolution,' she mused.

Bilqis had had ample opportunity and time to learn from her father and her tutors the art of statesmanship. Under the supervision of Sadik, she began to practice her talents and to flex her political muscles. With her exhilarating energy, her sense of adventure, and her youth, which was to her advantage, she finally convinced the council. Dubiously they relented and agreed to let her go.

"I will accompany you, my Queen," Sadik interjected when he saw she was determined to go. The nobles did not trust Queen Hagathia and Amenophis. The state left in their hands was not a welcomed idea. However, Sadik's intimidating look was more than enough to cut their arguments short.

Sadik had sustained a wound that left a scar on the right side of his neck. When irked the twitching of his ear, the scar all made his handsome dark face look even more fierce. His arresting looks were enhanced by his sharp and chiseled features, making his good looks even more pronounced. An imposing figure, with a deep respect for women, who pursued him unashamedly, the great warrior had never married. Instead, he had dedicated his entire life to the services of the royal family.

"I care about your safety, my Queen," when he saw she was about to protest, "as much as I did for your father's." The Queen would have preferred he stayed to protect the state and the palace. Her eyes filled with tenderness for the great warrior who, only to her, had become her gentle giant.

"Unless you stand and say 'Here I am Lord, send me,' there will be others who will sabotage your mission. There's an assignment only you can accomplish to save God's people.

The caravan route they were to travel was treacherous and notorious for its thieves and bandits. On the morning they were to embark on the long journey, the weather appeared ominous. It looked foreboding and was not suitable for travel as overhead the sky churned. Was it an omen, a bad sign? Dark clouds heavy with rain and edged in white threatened to release a ponderous storm. Lightning flashed, and the clouds overhead hung dark and heavy. Flashes and bolts of lightning suddenly unleashed a torrent of freezing rain, but that did not deter her.

Soon she was on her way accompanied by a retinue of servants, priests, and diplomats. The caravans and camels that left bearing spices, gold in abundance, precious stones, frankincense, bdellium, myrrh, balsam, and a wealth of many gifts were innumerable.

During the first lap of the journey, every time after setting up camp, each morning overwhelmed her. Opening her eyes to a new day, more tents, camels, and tribesmen would be sprawled across the plain waiting to escort her to king Solomon. Strong and valiant kin from neighboring villages had been hand-picked to accompany her joined her royal escort. At each stop, when they set up camp in the evenings, she held a meeting with the leaders. When approaching those within her inner circle, she made sure her gaze was unwavering, and her step did not falter, for she was not sure how they perceived her. At those moments when in counsel, she wondered if they thought they knew her as they always seemed to assess her with curiosity. She wondered if they saw her as their Queen because of her bloodline. Perhaps she was a gateway to the power they sought.

On the other hand, did they perceive her as a young Queen, capable or incapable of negotiating with a wise king? Or did they want her to see them and acknowledge their allegiance so she would remember them and their tribes with favor? Provoking thoughts absorbed her mind. 'I must never appear weak,' she thought as she began each meeting.

Not only will the storms of life challenge the course God has purposed for you, but challenges will come in all forms, shapes, and sizes, but women of destiny are not to be overcome by them.

Bilqis wondered in those sobering moments how a continent rich and overflowing with an abundance of natural resources had become so compromised. It was worth its weight in minerals and was the envy of other nations scrambling to solicit its riches at every opportunity. She, therefore, resolved to increase her knowledge not only from what she had learned from her father and tutors but with what she hoped to glean from the wise king she was soon to meet. She swore she would make it her duty to protect her kingdoms. Priority on her agenda would be to continue using the resources to raise the living standard to the highest quality for her people. Her focus was the continuance of an enriched state of power through the uninterrupted and unequaled quality of education.

And the pilfering which began continues into the 21st century as rich continents, because of political greed, corruption, and manipulation, have left people in dire straits, with no one to turn too. Unless the daughters of God step up and step out to take their rightful places in society, rulers of rich continents will continue to plunder, causing conflict and strife among the people. Meanwhile,

while the people turn on each other, the plundering of their
resources and the brain drain continues mercilessly.

Her Egypt was not only blessed with natural resources but
had rich fertile lands along the Nile River, which was the longest
river on earth. Its origins were in the great lakes of Central Africa
and Ethiopia, and it opened into the Nile River Delta along the
Mediterranean Coast. The advantage of the Nile River was that
each year, it rose independently and without failing, deposited a
mineral-rich, fine-grained type of soil. This sediment settled all
across the fields, eliminating the need for an irrigation system as
the river provided all the irrigation the soil required. Because of this
rich alluvial sediment deposited by the Nile River, the land had
become fertile, filled with green pastures, and it had the best and
largest palm forest in the world. She knew her father had fought
many battles to retain the hotly contested kingdoms. It was also
not just for the fertile valleys and resources, but for its easy
accessibility as a natural crossroads for the caravan routes between
the East and the West. It made the trade markets of the wealthy
buyers and sellers so much more convenient. Bilqis had decided she
was not going to let her kingdoms fall into the wrong hands.

PART TWO
The Queen of Sheba finally arrives in Israel

Song of Solomon

1 Kings 10:1-13; 9:5

Eventually, after months and months of travel, Manetho assured her they were only a couple of days away from their destination.

She had taken the journey fearlessly and had finally arrived. And what a display! The majestic escort of hundreds and hundreds of camels and caravans with beautifully adorned carriages were a sight to behold. One incomparable to the others carrying the Queen spilled over into the vast courtyard of king Solomon's palace. The Queen of Sheba came into the courts of king Solomon well-endowed in beauty and with carriages laden with her country's noblest gifts. The balance of the entourage stayed on the outskirts of the palace grounds awaiting further instructions on where to settle. The Queen's fiercest warriors were arrayed in their finest battle tunics as though going on a parade. They marched ahead of her carriage as she sat upright in the impressively adorned palanquin.

"My Queen," Sadik bowed low, "your father would have been very proud of you, if I may so. Your outward beauty surpasses all human understanding. None has been seen to match yours since the creation of man." It was the first time the great warrior had ever voiced a sentiment so endearing and personal before. The Queen heard the sincerity in his words and knew it had taken courage for him to address her with such a personal statement. Immediately her eyes filled with tears, but she held them back. She feared the kohl the maids had spent time applying around her eyes would run down her face. At that moment, the ache in her heart for her father was close to ripping it open.

"Thank you, Sadik. May we proceed?" was all she managed to whisper as a lump threatened to form in her throat.

She is lowered in her palanquin a little way from where the king stands.

71

Bilqis withheld a shudder as she realized she was laying eyes upon the king for the first time. It felt slightly exhilarating as her heart pounded against her chest.

"O great king Solomon, king of Israel," Sadik's voice boomed in the hushed silence. All eyes had turned to the palanquin anxious and excited to see the Queen step out of it.

"We greet you in the name of our Great God and your Great God, Yahweh. May we present to you our very own precious jewel and kinswoman Bilqis the Great Queen of Sheban and daughter of our Great God, Creator of Heaven and Earth."

She stepped out of the carriage. There was an audible awestruck admiration as the court bowed low. The king stood upright and unmoving, his eyes never leaving hers. She moved forward and looking up into his face, their eyes locked. She was glad of the thin veil that covered her face because he could not see the flush that instantly rose.

"Welcome to Israel, Queen of Sheban," he greeted her loudly for the audience to hear and stretched out his hand.

She had mixed feelings when hearing his voice for the first time. She had expected a much deeper voice, more baritone like her fathers' had been, or even like Sadik's. Instead, although strong and very masculine, it had an amazingly rich and pleasant sound to it.

She placed her hand in his, and he whispered for her ears only.

"Just I have dreamt and imagined. You have ravished my heart, and I have longed for this moment."

Her heart did a skip as it pounded against her chest. She feared he would hear it as he stood so close. The king was indeed a very good looking man and yes, ever so charming, a mirror reflection of his poetic letters. At that moment, it was as if those letters she had read and re-read through nights of wondering who and what he looked like were coming alive.

Composing herself, she immediately called to mind the purpose of the mission. Top of the agenda was to negotiate the ship and port terms of agreement. She forewarned herself to be wary for she knew him not. Except what she had heard about him, and the words written in his letters, she concluded was not enough. Seeing face to face was a reality. She wondered if he would pursue her in person as he had in his letters. Or were his letters a snare to get her to come to Israel? Had she fallen into the trap? All sorts of doubts began to plague her. 'This is not the time to entertain these cheerless thoughts,' she told herself. She jolted her thoughts to the present scenario that was evolving before her.

In the days to follow, she witnessed for herself the king's charm and the wealth of his kingdom, which had become legendary. Now he was preparing to mount a maritime expedition to add to the prosperity of his kingdom. 'My presence here is to secure my kingdoms share in the proposed new sea route," she told herself, 'and nothing more.'

After the first meeting, she asked for a week's respite following their arduous journey. She also needed time to filter through the emotional turmoil she was experiencing. Conflicting thoughts were running through her mind. She began to wonder if she had made a wise decision or a foolish one by coming to the king personally.

After two weeks of not being summoned to his presence to begin the discussions, she began to feel anxious. She called for her maidservants and Sadik. Also summoned were Medinet Habu, the high priest, and the commander of the regiment.

"Listen to me all of you," she said, once they were all assembled. "We are not here on a pleasure cruise, and we are not here in a palace of an altruistic and charitable king. We barely know him, his ways, nor his people. We are here on trade negotiations. So you all have to present yourselves in a dignified and professional manner at all times."

Discussed with much deliberation was the conduct expected from them.

Only Sadik remained after everyone had departed. He wanted to know what she had meant by the statement, 'We barely know him, his ways nor his people.'

"Well, we have much to learn about the king, his people, and during these transactions and terms of the alliance, anything can happen."

"I don't understand," said Sadik, sensing there was more to what she was saying but was deliberately hedging.

She knew he wanted her to elaborate. Afraid she'd reveal the conflicting feelings she was having towards the king, she cut him short.

"Trust me, Sadik," she said, dismissing him.

"Very well, my Queen," he said, bowing low. He exited from the elegant chambers the king had graciously assigned for her use during her stay.

It was into the second week; just when she was about to send word to him regarding the purpose of their mission, she received a message. He had set a date for the first formal negotiating meeting. After that, in the days that followed, it was business as usual.

They had been at the palace about a month when his charming poetic notes began. And so began the cold war between submitting to the king's charisma or letting her guard down. Without the alliance proposal she had at least expected, she refused to give in to his wooing. She equally refused to be treated like a Queen who did not put the interest of her people and vision for her kingdoms first. She had to be recognized and appreciated as one whose own desires were secondary. The needs and welfare of her people and the nations she had been called to serve were her primary objectives.

"Now that my eyes have gazed upon your beautiful face, I have seen you are indeed dark and lovely to behold. I have compared you, my love for my filly among Pharaoh's chariots. Your cheeks are lovely with ornaments, your neck with chains of gold. Song of Solomon 1:5

Did he indeed compare her to his wives and concubines? And did he think he could continue wooing her with his love songs?

One night she had had enough. In frustration, she grabbed the stylus and began to write furiously on the parchment before she changed her mind.

"Until the day breaks and the shadows flee away, I will go my way to the mountain of myrrh and to the hill of frankincense, from whence I come." Song of Solomon 4:6

She waited eagerly for a reply, but to her dismay, nothing came, and neither did he request her presence for further trade talks.

It was a week later, after receiving her note that he responded. With trembling hands, she opened the long-awaited reply.

"There are sixty queens and eighty concubines and virgins without number. My dove, my perfect one, is the only one of her mother, the fathers of the one who bore her. The daughters saw her and called her blessed, the queens and concubines, and they praised her. Who is she who looks forth as the morning, fair as the moon, clear as the sun, awesome as an army with banners." Song of Solomon 6:8-10

This time she did not respond hastily for this note struck a chord as memories of her dear mother came flooding into her mind.

She sent for Medinet-Habu, the high priest, in search of answers to the many questions that had been afflicting her heart. And she saw he had none when he answered;

"Matters of the heart my Queen are between you and the one who pursues you."

Of course, this did not still the rapid beating of her heart when she set eyes on him, nor ease the restless and sleepless nights knowing he was so close yet so far away. She would lie awake at night, the longing in her heart burning an unquenchable flame. She prayed to God for strength until she would fall into a restless sleep. After a while, she removed the small gold artifacts on her dressing table and just left the picture of her mother and father. And from that day, she no longer requested the services of Medinet-Habu, the high priest. She had to get back to hearing from God herself as before.

When the king realized there was no forthcoming response to his last note, he instead sent her an invitation to dine alone with him.

"Make me extra beautiful tonight," she said to Faridah, her maidservant.

"Oh my Queen," she said, "you are true without any doubt the most beautiful Queen I've ever seen, and you will always be beautiful." Nevertheless, the maid adorned the Queen's neck with jewels and ornaments from her mother's collection, and chains of gold from the abundance of the riches of Sheban.

The Queen had been assigned personal chambers because of the nature of the mission. Purely trade negotiations. But word soon got to the king's wives and his concubines that their king was in love with the new visitor. Jealousy and envy flared up as they began to whine of being deprived of the king's affections. The king's glittering harem was full of suspicious eunuchs, maidservants, slaves, and perfumed bejeweled concubines. But even with all the complaints and rivalry, the Queen was not prepared to play a concubine role to the king.

The king was smitten with her. The love becomes obvious even to the blindest person in the king's palace. As an excuse to see her, he begins to seek her input in the affairs of the state. But the Queen also enjoys these sessions. She's particularly drawn to the similarities between the literary work composed by the scribe Amenemope that she had studied. These coincided with the king's wisdom he executed during disputes. His Meshalim (this was a set of rules he had received by divine revelation from his God. It was a guidebook which he had to use to rule and reign over Israel). This set of rules was authoritative sayings and were guidelines for man's behavior, civil, moral, and religious actions that were to be adhered too.

Before leaving her country, the Queen had looked forward to the letters from the king. These had been delivered by her trusted trader Manetho when he returned from Israel and other faraway regions. The Queen had also been curious not only about his fame, but the fame concerning the Name of the Lord. The Name of the Lord was also one of the reasons that had attracted her and had piqued her interest. She had heard how he spent seven years building the temple for his Lord. The time he had invested in the preparations was admirable. The leadership skills applied in accomplishing what He had, were phenomenal. The money spent, his commitment, and dedication were outstanding. She couldn't help thinking of the number of years it had taken her people to build the Great Pyramids and obelisk that were the pride of her nation. Nothing equivalent or close to her nation's heritage had been seen, discovered, or ever built.

In the months that followed at every opportunity, the king sought the Queen's company. Once the court proceedings settled for the day, he would take her on a guided tour of the temple he had built for his God. He explained that God had forbidden his father, King David, to build it, having shed too much blood during his battles.

Instead, God had appointed him. He enjoyed the pleasure of giving her the step by step instructions he had received on how to build it.

"We have many temples, obelisk, and pyramids," the Queen had said with pride. "So why does your God only want one temple?"

"Our God is jealous because He is the creator of all things. He does not want what He has created to take pre-eminence above Himself. He also does not appreciate being equaled to what He has created. Neither does He appreciate 'it' being held in higher esteem than Himself. Above all, He abhors being set or compared in the same standing to what man has created with his hands.

The Queen was silent for a moment as she pondered on the king's words. After a while, she admitted that Manetho had aroused her curiosity when he told her about the temple the king had built for his God. The first day he took her to the temple she saw;

1 Kings 10:5b ..."his entryway by which he went up to the house of the Lord, there was no more spirit in her."

She was indeed overly impressed. She saw the quality of the material the king had used to build the temple of the Lord. The building of the temple included where he had sought assistance, labor force he used, and the delegation of the workload. He had made His laborers work in shifts. He combined excellent management, leadership, and supervision technics. To accomplish the best-finished work, he had sought assistance outside the known and familiar, outside his environment and kingdom. A replica of works of craft from her land greeted her. The obvious wisdom in some of the works and designs imported from her Egypt was strikingly evident. And she smiled as she thought and marveled at the opportunities trading provided.

The Queen was left flabbergasted by the construction of the temple. She was particularly intrigued by his strength in the ability to meet the conditions stipulated by his God. She wanted to know how he had developed the characteristics of a strong and wise leader that reminded her so much of her father. The king did not hesitate to disclose the Lord's promises.

Taking her by the hand, he said, "come." The king led her to a cubicle from where he extracted a scroll. He opened to a section where his scribes had written the instructions he had received from the Lord.

1 Kings 10:12 "Concerning this temple which you are building, if you walk in My statutes, execute my judgments, keep all my commandments, and walk in them, then I will perform My word with you, which I spoke to your father, David."

"Is this what your God told you?"

"Yes," said the king. "These were the steps related to the work I was about to execute. They would ultimately affect the involvement and everything concerning the team. These were the people I was preparing for God's kingdom. All this would depend on my ability to be of strong character and an example into those I was imparting. And the success would be dependent on following the conditions stipulated by my God. And if I succeeded, He would perform His word."

"And what were the conditions," asked the Queen.

"I was to obey His statutes, be wise in executing His judgments, and I was to show no partiality. I was to keep His word with no compromise, and I was to walk in His ways. Then the Lord said, *'I will keep my end of the bargain, I will perform my word, the prophetic word spoken over you.'* So before making any demands about walking with the Lord on the people I was to live by His word. I was to do what he commanded me concerning the building of His temple. Most importantly, I was to execute righteous judgment for the people.

An end came to her guided tour of the temple. In the days and months that followed, she was able to see that the temple he had built was a spiritual house, the building of God's people. The foundation laid, and the stones used to build them were God's word. Godly character and Godly principles were to fashion the people.

She understood that the 'food' on the table was the diverse teachings from the scrolls, the intercession, the prayers, the praise, and worship. The seating of the servants was the different positions of leadership qualities they had. Being extracted from the people in his assembly was their good qualities. The apparel, the different clothing that they wore, was no longer external but internal clothing of compassion, mercy, love, kindness, and self-control, etc. expressed outwardly in servanthood. His cupbearers were the fulfilling and the carrying out of the gifting and offices his most trusted men possessed. She observed their entryway by which they went up to the house of the Lord. They entered and went up into His presence through prayer, praise and worship, and the reading of the scrolls.

'But this is what my father and his ancestors before him have done and continue to do,' the Queen thought. She believed some of what she was witnessing was a replication of the ancient Egyptian works done by her people.'

1) She saw the quality of material used to build a lasting relationship with the Lord. He had invested in quality spiritual learning,

2) The labor force he had engaged had a positive influence in his life,

3) Allocation of time for each workload, i.e., business, ministry, personal, had been delegated for each area,

4) Accountability of those under his management and supervision. He managed and supervised living temples of the Lord, knowing he was building for the service of the Lord.

"And then I prayed and said, 'And now I pray, O God of Israel, let Your word come true, which You have spoken to Your servant David, my father.'"

"And have you lived according to what He commanded you?" the Queen asked as they slowly walked through the temple.

"Yes, our Jehovah allows us to reason with Him and to hold Him accountable to His word. So I beseeched Him not to look at my flaws, of which I have many," the king confessed.

"Scripture says in *Isaiah 1:18 relates, 'Come now, let us reason together,' says the Lord.* And I said, 'now that the temple is complete, *'let Your word come true.'* And at the same time, I wondered!

1 Kings 8:27 "But will God indeed dwell on the earth? Behold, heaven and the heaven of heavens cannot contain You. How much less this temple which I have built!

And I was humbled by the fact that God would want to dwell among His people, mere mortals and I said"

1 Kings 8:28 Yet regard the prayer of Your servant and his supplication...'

"I beseeched Him to consider His people in a particular way, to gaze at them specially, pay attention to them, and to have a high opinion and esteem them highly as His chosen people."

"Had you or your people failed in obeying God, then what would have happened?" the Queen gently probed.

"I said Lord," *1 Kings 8:29 'that Your eyes be open towards them day and night so that You hear them day and night and act accordingly whether it is to bless or punish them, You forgive.'*

Today the responsibility is upon individuals as well as leaders and intercessors to pray for one another and the children of God, strengthening the hands that hang down and the feeble knees. Only through prayer does God act on behalf of His children

"I implored Him and said,"

1 Kings 8:34 'He must act,'

"He was to bring them back on the right course. Or there would be dire consequences, and we would be in serious trouble."

1 Kings 8:35 'When the heavens are shut, and there is no rain.'

"That's when the blessings ceased. There was no more revelation. Instead, there was more strife, and we knew there was a grave sin in the land. I summoned all the leaders of all the tribes and families, and we assembled in Jerusalem. Together with the entire communities, we sacrificed sheep and oxen in such numbers; nobody could keep count. And when we had repented we prayed, and I prayed,"

1 Kings 8:36 'Then hear, open the windows of heaven and teach them the good way in which they should walk...'

And when we obeyed, He said,"

1 Kings 9:5 "Then I will establish the throne of your kingdom over Israel forever, as I promised David your father, saying, "You shall not fail to have a man on the throne of Israel."

Because God knows His plan for our lives, He puts His seal upon those who will extend His Kingdom on earth without compromise. From King David's children, He chose Solomon God knew he would not compromise on the best material for the building of the temple. Building God's temple in this dispensation is the building of God's people.

God will establish our households so that there will always be born again Christians in the family. They would take the baton passed on from the previous generation and pass it on to the next generation. As long as the kingdom principles and the ways of God in the family, land, business, etc. are maintained, adhered to, followed and practiced, we shall not fail to have a son/daughter and a ruler on the throne of God's kingdom.

It was at this juncture that the Queen remembered her conversations with Amarna the eunuch while he lay on his recovery bed after the attempted kidnapping episode.

Thank goodness for his screams that had alerted the palace guards. They had come running down the hallway to her chambers. On hearing the pounding of the guard's boots, the would-be kidnappers had escaped through her bedroom window, making their getaway through the palace gardens.

The princess had visited Amarna every day until he had fully recovered. It was during one of those visits; the princess noted that Amarna only used natural herbs for his wounds and had continuously read from the book, Scroll of Life.

During their many conversations, he had proudly related his family's history and how the belief had been passed on from generation to generation. Coming from a lineage of eunuchs, he had plenty to share. According to Amarna, all his ancestors had undertaken the long journey from Ethiopia to worship in Jerusalem. Each eunuch had had a personal encounter and a visitation from God. However, one remarkable story had stood out for Amarna and had had a lasting impression upon him. The story was about a particular eunuch. The eunuch baptized in a nearby river along the road on his way to Jerusalem was an incredible story.

"Why has he had such a major impact on you?" the princess asked.

"Because after the baptism, the Spirit of the Lord took the servant of God who had baptized him away and transported him to another location."

However, after Amarna's recovery, they had little opportunity to talk, and conversations had ceased.

Then one day, during the tour of the temple with the king, the Queen experienced a 'light bulb moment.' Suddenly the reality of Amarna's stories and the king's made sense as an internal transformation began to take place. She realized that the king's God, Amarna's God and her God was a covenant-keeping God for He had never failed any of them. There had always been a son/daughter to continue serving Him, and He, in turn, continued to bless them, their households, and their nations. At that moment, she knew she was going to bear a son to continue the lineage of her kingdoms. Just as she, her father and ancestors, spoke and heard from their God, her son would also walk and talk to God, the Great Creator.

Chapter 9:5 "Then I will establish the throne of your kingdom over Israel forever, as I promised David your father, saying, "You shall not fail to have a man on the throne of Israel."

The queen felt a special fondness for Amarna. She felt more drawn to the king every time she had toured the temple with him.

The related story told to the princess by Amarna is a replica of Acts 8:26-39

After the temple tours, the queen began to have a change of heart. Spending more and more time together, she began to soften under the king's attention. When separated, she responded to his love poems more endearingly.

No longer able to restrain himself, and overwhelmed by his love for her, the king had finally proposed.

The wedding preparations began in earnest. Finally, the long-awaited wedding day was upon them. For the Queen, Sadik, and Faridah, it was a heart-stirring day. But her other maidservants who had accompanied her were over the moon. They had worked the previous night and half of the following day preparing her. A scented body bath, followed by a scented oil body massage, had left her skin feeling soft and supple. The next morning while some wove beads and pearls through her long black hair, others worked on her hands and feet. Rubbing and massaging more scented oils, they painted them with special nail paints specially made for the Queen.

When she stepped out, all present within her inner court were left enthralled by her beauty. A boisterous crowd of locals had gathered early outside the palace walls. All they wanted was to get a glimpse of her knowing she would pass by on her way to the royal wedding chapel. The thin veil covering her head barely concealed her face because her beauty still seeped through, leaving her audience gasping in unabashed admiration.

The beautiful carriage with an interior upholstered in delicate white satin was part of the wedding gift from the king. Sadik, appointed to be the 'Bride's Escort,' occupied the head coach that was pulled by horses draped in a beautiful purple cloth. Medinet-Habu, the High Priest, invited to the ceremony as a witness to the marriage, sat at his side. The king had proposed his priest conduct the ceremony. He wished to claim the Queen as his wife according to the Israeli tradition. The marriage had also been officiated under the customs of Israel. However, after participating in the festivities, a small private traditional celebration was enjoyed by the Queen and her people.

Exhibiting great strength, a woman of power, and endowed with elegance, the Queen of Sheba possessed a fascination for the opposite gender. Even when she walked, it was with ethereal poise and grace. Now she seemed to float as she walked towards the king on the arm of her protector, Sadik. Sadik wore the traditional royal wedding regalia that her father would have worn. At the opposite end, the king stood regal and tall also in the impressive royal bridegroom attire. He was transfixed as he watched in awe at the beautiful figure approaching him.

"I am lovesick," Song of Solomon 2:5b, the king, whispered into her ear, making her blush as he removed the veil from her face.

The ceremony and celebrating lasted well into the night. Finally, the king bade the remaining guests goodnight, and he and the Queen departed to his chambers.

That night as the doors opened into his chambers, the music that greeted them, the lute, harp, the flute, and other stringed instruments filled the room with a melody that soothed and refreshed their souls.

"The last song," said the king to the lead musician. The Queen picked up a fig from a large fruit bowl on the table and popped it into his mouth. Leading her onto the floor in a slow waltz, the two seem to mesh into one body and spirit.

"Sustain me with cakes of raisins, refresh me with apples, for I am lovesick," he whispered into ear. *Song of Solomon 2:5*

A MEMORABLE NIGHT

Bilqis's mother, Queen Ismenie, was a beautiful woman who had used her beauty as a gift to charm her husband king Agabos. She had kept him captivated by her wisdom and beauty. One of her mesmerizing and enchanting devices was to dance and twirl around and around before him. She wore gold and silver bracelets and bangles around her wrist and ankles that jingled with every leap, stamping of her feet and the clapping of her hands. Sometimes it was her bewitching smile and then a serious look that fascinated him. The jingling of her jewels exemplified her femininity and had the king eating out of her hand. And now those moves and lessons were coming into effect as the Queen of Sheba danced before King Solomon. She pushed the death of her beloved mother to the back of her mind, a mother and a friend who had taught her to dance, laugh, and sing.

"His left hand is under my head, and his right-hand embraces me." Songs of Solomon 2:6

84

That night, Menelik, their son, was conceived.

Since their marriage, the king had not left her side. But all of a sudden, without any explanation, he stopped coming to her chambers at the end of each day. It was now two weeks since she had last seen him. Had he already tired of her? Just when she had this incredible news to tell him, he went quiet on her. The last message she had received was that he was busy, and he would see her as soon as he was free. But in the past as busy as he had been, he had spent every night with her. What had changed? Not knowing what was going on left her feeling more alone and even more vulnerable than ever.

The Queen walked slowly towards the huge windows, overlooking a courtyard. Nestled below was a pool surrounded by an enchanting flower garden. It sent its reflection rippling through the wind that carried the scent of its lovely flowers from below. But tonight, the Queen was oblivious to the beauty beneath her windows. Nor did she delight in the perfumed air that tried to invade her disturbing thoughts with its fragrance. She had to see the king. 'I will go and see the king even though I know it's against the law if not summoned,' she concluded. Her mind made up, the next morning she called for Faridah. "Please withhold my meals for the next three days and three nights."

"Do you plan to go on a fast, my Queen," asked Faridah.

"Yes, Faridah," the Queen replied, "three days and three nights."

"Very well, my Queen, I will get all the other maids to join us." Faridah knew without being told that when the Queen fasted, it was the norm for her and the other maids to fast and pray with her.

After three days and three nights, the Queen summoned for Sadik and told him to escort her to the king.

"I need to see the king," she said.

"What troubles, my Queen?" Sadik asked with concern when he saw the apprehension on her face.

"Nothing that I cannot handle," she replied shortly.

"Very well, my Queen, I will send word to the king."

Midday, the king, was ready to receive her. She put on her royal robes and left her chambers with Sadik by her side. They were met by the king's royal guards who politely ushered them through the hallway to the Hall Of Judgement. The guard opened the doors, and she stood in the outer court facing him. The king was sitting on his royal throne facing the entrance of the Hall. She hesitated for a moment because he was in counsel with his advisors, but as soon as he saw her, he dismissed them. The king held out his golden scepter that was in his hand.

"Come forward, my Queen," he called out to her.

The guard stepped aside, and she was led forward by Sadik. She curtsied then stood upright facing him. Stepping forward she reached out and touched the top of the scepter.

"What is your wish my Queen, what is your request? Ask, and whatever you wish will be given to you," said the king. There was a slight knowing, mischievous smirk at the corners of his mouth that the Queen did not miss.

"If it pleases, the king, let the king come to my chambers for a message that I wish to deliver in person."

'Here we go.' the king thought, but merely replied, "as you wish my Queen, I shall come."

"Thank you, my king." She gave him a haughty look, curtsied, turned, and was led away by Sadik.

In the evening, when the king entered her chambers, she had her back to the door. Seeing the outline of her delicate figure through the fine transparent linen gown, he was mesmerized. The white gown she was wearing was ankle length and accentuated her olive skin and the darkness of her hair. Enraptured, he couldn't help thinking that she was lovely. She was a healthy woman with an unblemished elegance. Her radiance was striking with an irresistible allure that left him weak at the knees. 'Shameful,' he thought as he straightened his back, 'I'm a man of great power, a king for goodness sake.'

She turned to face him, he sighed deeply, charmed by the figure before him. Her black hair pulled back African style, and her eyes rimmed in black kohl encased remarkably long lashes.

"Your two breasts are like two fawns, Twins of a gazelle, which feed among the lilies." Song of Solomon 4:5

"Your breasts" were the first words he uttered as he stepped towards her.

"And you are indeed the son of a shepherd." As irate and anxious as she was, the Queen couldn't help smiling at his greeting, portraying her breasts as fawns, lovely, perfect, and fresh. The king was forever captivated as he slowly advanced towards her.

"You have ravished my heart, my sister, my spouse, You have ravished my heart with one look of your eyes, With one link of your necklace." Song of Solomon 4:9

"But you have kept away from me for two weeks without any explanation."

'By night on my bed, I sought the one I love, I sought him, but I did not find him. I will arise now, I said...' Song of Solomon 3: 2a,"

The Queen retorted the smile leaving her face, "so stop it, my king, I have something of importance to share with you."

Two months after their wedding night, when she discovered she was pregnant, she had at first been anxious and had assessed the situation with a hint of trepidation. The day she requested his presence, when he came to her chambers, she tried to hide her displeasure with him. However, despite her low spirits, when she conveyed the news about the pregnancy, to her relief, the king was elated. Her annoyance turned to pleasure when he received the news with excitement and enthusiasm.

He gazed at her lovingly. It was hard for him to believe that she was pregnant. Her figure had remained sublime, majestic, as though untouched and unmarked by her very first pregnancy.

In the days that followed, the king made up for neglecting her. He made sure he lavished her with more attention so as not to distress her.

"Come with me from Lebanon, my spouse. Look from the top of Amana, from the top of Sinai and Hermon. From the lion's dens, From the mountains of the leopards." Song of Solomon 4:8 entreated the Queen one night.

"I cannot," the king said in exasperation. It was obvious they had had the conversation before, and it was a subject the king did not enjoy discussing.

"What's to become of us now that I am with child? Surely you can rule and reign over the two dynasties which will be united by our son," she tried to persuade him.

"I cannot, the Lord has called me to govern Israel. Our son will become the king of your kingdoms, and he will be part of my family, your family, therefore of a divine lineage. Honor, and reverential respect; tributes rightfully fit for a king will be paid to him. Besides," the king continued trying to appease her. "Would you have him endangered as my other sons oppose him for the crown after my death even if I leave him as my successor?" The Queen bowed her head, turned her back to him, but not before he saw the tears of frustration and disappointment.

"Listen to me please, my beloved," said the king, coming up behind her. He tried to enfold her in his arms, but the Queen pulled away.

"You are the most powerful and richest king in the world. You can do as you please, you don't want to, is that not the truth?" she said, raising her voice. The influence of her mother's native blood was beginning to show as her cheeks flushed, and her lips trembled.

"Why don't you try to understand?" The king walked towards her and tried to embrace her once again. "Are you not happy with the decisions I've made for both you and the child?"

"And need I remind you my king that my kingdoms have dominion and hold the monopoly over the spice route. In my own right, I have a wealthy, influential and powerful monarchy. During my father's reign, our kingdoms were superpowers, and they still are. The surrounding neighbors look to us as a role model. They hope to imitate our wealth, influence and power. So do not tell me how noble and generous you have been to our child and me."

"I have done what I think is right just for you and the child. He is my son, he will be part of my family and yours and will be of a unique divine lineage. He will be the king of both kingdoms as you are, and you will be regent until he becomes of age. I will make sure your throne is secured. You will be protected, and homage paid to both of you. The ring, which is the family heirloom, will be a symbol of his birthright. At eighteen, when he returns, he will take possession of the most sacred and revered treasure, "The Ark Of The Covenant." Fortunately, he refrained from blurting out that his kingdom would have had the monopoly had they not signed the sea route agreement. He had learned that his little Queen could be quite a spitfire when angered. He had seen how she stood up for herself when jealously attacked by the other wives. Needless to say, when her servants were threatened or mistreated, smoldering anger erupted. He didn't want to arouse her anger any further, especially in her current condition.

"Begone, my king, I wish to be alone," she said, dismissing him.

"Don't you appreciate anything I have done?" the king asked in indignation. "I've gone against the officials, against the governors and my people. I have boasted of your quick and aristocratic mind and your diplomatic approach to all your subjects. But above your intelligence, my beloved," said the king, trying to soften his tone, "I'm enthralled by your love for the language of our love songs. I love how you transcribe and your sultry articulation, like no other maiden I've ever known."

"How noble of you, my king, now if you don't mind, I wish to be alone," she said, turning her back to him.

"As you wish, my Queen. Goodnight," the king replied and walked promptly to the door. For a second, he hesitated at the doorway, then turning around, he said, "I'll be back to see you as soon as you have calmed down," and walked out, shutting the door behind him.

With the negotiations settled, the trade agreements signed, and sealed; the Queen knew there was nothing else she could say to persuade the king to go with her. His ability to reign and extend his influence over the combined kingdoms would have finally taken its toll on him. She had also begun to worry incessantly about the affairs of her kingdoms back home, and so she wisely relinquished her position and decided to return. Besides, they had agreed Menelik was old enough to travel.

But before leaving, she had other matters to settle. Initially there had been strife between her and the other wives and concubines. However, many came to respect her when they saw they could not intimidate her. She had befriended several, and a few had confided in her. They confessed that they no longer wished to be in the king's harem as they were still young enough to wed. She approached the king with the petition asking for their release. The Queen set a precedent by persuading the king to release those who felt they could still live their own lives outside the harem. If they chose to leave the harem, the king was to grant them their freedom. The Queen even went further to argue their cases, stating that not only was he to grant them their wishes, but he was to release them with a dowry.

The Queen had learned from her own experience the unjust treatment of being a female when she had ascended the throne. She understood the persecution women had endured throughout the centuries. Male domination had been perpetuated throughout human history, propagating a lie that devalued females. This deception projected women as mere objects favoring the masculine as stronger and, therefore, more superior. She remembered in one of her lectures the stories that Christianity had waged a campaign of propaganda against women. This campaign had demonized intelligently, and freethinking queens and ordinary women. Women burned at the stakes those deemed witches. As much as she loved the king, she felt the male ego had run unchecked by their female counterparts for far too long. Well, she decided she was going to put an end to this injustice. The day she had been crowned Queen, the pendulum had swung in favor of women.

She used the same strategies he had used to woo her in his poetic discourse. She pointed out his tribute to women, whom he had likened to an enclosed garden. Unfulfilled, their God-given potential would not be released. Releasing them, she argued, they would be free to blossom, realize their life's calling, pursue their dreams, and would bear much good fruit. The king had put up a fight as he thought her demands were unreasonable. Using all the persuading skills inherited from Achsah, she had eventually won as he finally relented and caved to her demands. When persuading the king to release some of his concubines, she held him accountable to his word in the rhapsody he had composed. In it, he had combined her natural fragrance of a loving and giving soul with her nurturing spirit as an intricate part of God's creation within the spices. He defended his belief to be the vital and fundamental part of nature without which humanity would not survive.

Song of Solomon 4:12-16 'A garden enclosed, is my sister, my spouse,
A spring shut up, a fountain sealed.
Your plants are an orchard of pomegranates with pleasant fruits,
With pleasant fruits, Fragrant henna with spikenard.
Spikenard and saffron,
Calamus and cinnamon.
With all trees of frankincense, myrrh, and aloes.
With all chief spices.
A fountain of gardens,
A well of living waters,
And streams from Lebanon.

"Oh yes," said the king with a twinkle in his eyes. Once again, he began to serenade her with his love words, but the Queen had a counter-attack as they began to banter back and forth. The Queen was able to reveal the value and the purpose of God's creation in the usage of the spices and the importance of releasing them for humanity through women;

"A garden enclosed is my sister, my spouse, a spring shut up, A garden fountain sealed." 4:12

And of what use will she be all sealed up," said the Queen. "You have likened her to a garden, a beautiful garden, my king, producing beauty to behold and vegetation for man's consumption. But shut up and sealed, it is confined. Preventing it from flowing stops nature from taking its course. A garden-likened to women who suppressed smothers her inner creativity and inhibits what would be the beautiful outer manifestations."

"But my love," said the king,

"Your plants are an orchard of pomegranates, with pleasant fruit, fragrant henna with spikenard." 4:13

*"Spikenard with saffron, calamus with cinnamon, with all trees of frankincense, myrrh, and aloes, with all the chief spices"*4:14

"Is it not for my pleasure, my healing balms for my wearied soul, for my eyes to gaze and feast upon?" replied the king.

"But released, she is a fountain in a garden, able to influence multitudes, producing more offshoots, an influence on the young branches/generations. She is a wellspring of living waters, the very purpose of her existence.

"A fountain of gardens, a well of living waters, and streams from Lebanon," 4:15 said the Queen.

4:16 Awake, O north wind, and come O south, blow upon my garden, that its spices may flow out, Let my beloved come to his garden and eat its pleasant fruits."

It's a reciprocal benefit. By your encouragement, as you blow upon a woman's garden, the woman flourishes.

"And should you hold back or restrain, it withers away, my king. Don't you see, likening her to a garden which is the ground adjoining a house, used for growing flowers, herbs, and spices, fruit, and vegetables, and all things wonderful. Or she can be an ornamental ground used for public enjoyment; the ground all laid on. Release them so that from their fertile soil, they can sustain those that are dependent upon them. They will be the ground that is adjoined and attached to their homes, their environments, communities, and nations. Out of her ground, she shall yield forth and increase in fruit. She'll be a fruitful vine, bearing the fruit of the ground, nourishing the earth, as well as bearing the fruit of the Spirit. At liberty, she will release the beautiful fruit within her," said the Queen. *"The fruit of the Spirit; love, joy, peace, long-suffering, kindness, goodness, faithfulness, gentleness, and self-control." Galatians 5:22*

"Mmm," said the king before he continued. "I see your point of view. She is the outward physical beauty reflecting the flower garden that beautifies the surroundings. Her inner spiritual beauty lights up the natural environment and surroundings wherever she goes and whatever she does. Indeed she is the garden that yields and produces herbs for healing. She is the breath of life to the perishing world; she's a light of the world."

"O my love, you are as beautiful as Tirzah lovely as Jerusalem, awesome as an array with banners. 6:4

And a witty and wise one too," said the king. "She is indeed a beautiful vegetable and herb garden that brings nourishment, nutrients for the body, herbs, and spices for healing, sweet-smelling perfume, for delight," continued the king.

"Yes, yes, my king," said the Queen. "She also reflects an ornamental ground used for enjoyment. Her gifts and talents are not to be hidden under a bushel but used as gifts to be seen, explored, and encouragement. And her inner and outer beauty is not to be flaunted but to be admired as one who carries and utilizes it for the Lord.

On the other hand, a garden enclosed is one surrounded or closed off on all sides, fenced-in to make it private property. I dare say that is not your Lord's intention. And my king, if a garden is closed off, or fenced in, or used only as private property, then it cannot produce or yield what it carries within to its fullest potential. It is limited, the roots are constrained and cannot spread out.

What's supposed to produce or yield forth, growth stunted, hampered, retarded, restricted, a severe and negative impact on nature. The restriction applies in the spiritual as well as in the natural. If the garden is enclosed– (a visionless life) it's immature, will produce and yield dwarfs, strife, envy, jealousy, low self-esteem. Lack of purpose and all negativity around her will finally takes its toll on her and those around her.

All that a garden can produce, what it offers to sustain life cannot grow, spring forth because there is no water to water it. When suppressed, the spring is unable to gush or flow out. The fountain is sealed, isolated, impervious, not allowing the fluid to pass through into the garden; that is, women abuse and love restrained, my king."

EPILOGUE

Because of the complexities of the numerous challenges women sometimes face, it's easier to yield to the mold society prescribes. Subtle handicaps in the guise of conformity, complacency, familiarity, environmental and mental conditioning, etc. can become clutches that they consciously or unconsciously begin to lean on. These ingrained belief systems, instead of being a challenge to overcome, can become comforting refuges. Applying anything else to resist these bondages becomes mentally and physically exerting and distressing.

As intellectual beings created in God's image, we do not need to succumb to these so-called 'reassuring sensations.' If and when we do, we forsake the activation of our God-given conceptual and creative abilities. Instead, we allow life's oppressive circumstances to think, and to 'do' for us. When this occurs, we lean on the ideologies and opinions of the world to direct us instead of turning to God, the creator.

Allowing the Holy Spirit to teach, counsel, and guide us, He clarifies and brings to light and life great revelations of the Bible's contents. Therefore these bible stories, when processed through the eye of the Holy Spirit within, are not only interesting but thought-provoking. Propelling one forward into one's purpose and destiny, they come to life. Revealing the nuggets of the hidden treasures of heaven only to people who are willing and are prepared to penetrate and diligently study these texts.

The Queen of Sheba had to venture further afield to seek and to glean certain skills to enhance her own for the sake of her kingdoms. She embarked on a life-changing journey being a leader summoned to shape the events and history of her nations. To accomplish the kingdom protocol as well as to effect the changes we desire to see, we have to lead the way. One can lead from a position of weakness to one of strength that the Lord gives you.

IN CONCLUSION

The Lord becomes our beloved, and we say;

"Come blow upon my garden that its spices may flow…"
Song of Solomon 4:16

"Come blow Your Holy Spirit upon my garden (life) that its spices (Your love) may flow (show). Out of my garden (life), let nutrients that nourish the soul and pleasant fragrance permeate the atmosphere.

With fervent, intense, and passionate prayer, we will awaken and cause the treasures in the storeroom of heaven to open up and blow upon our lives, letting spices (love) flow out, utilizing the gifts, talents, skills, potentials, etc., embedded within.

"Let my beloved come to his garden and eat of its fruit," *Song of Solomon 4:16*

Let the Holy Spirit that abides within come into every circumstance, every situation of life. And eat of its fruit, delighting in the life-producing work of our hands for family, friends, community, and nations, etc. and glorify His Name as fruits, of love, peace, joy, long-suffering, goodness, patience, gentleness, kindness, faithfulness are manifest.

8

JUST A MAIDSERVANT

BUT WITH A PURPOSE

2 KINGS 5

In 2 Kings 5:1-9, we read the story of Naaman and a maidservant who are the primary protagonists in this narrative.

In this chapter, the entire tale is narrated to capture the ethos of God's healing process. Despite the handicap or an abyss of pain and suffering one may find oneself in, it does not negate the fact that we have all been created with a purpose to fulfill. To achieve this purpose to its fullest potential, God has not left anyone disadvantaged. Because it's a spiritual mandate with a physical manifestation, He has also equipped us with spiritual tools, one being 'the spirit of boldness.'

2 Tim 1:7 For the Lord has not given us a spirit of fear, but of boldness of power and of love and of a sound mind.

Prov 28:1 The wicked flee when no man pursues, but the righteous are as bold as a lion.

While Naaman was engaged in physical warfare, winning battles and conquering nations, God promoted women to conquer in the spiritual realm. He orchestrated the services of a married woman, Naaman's wife, and a young girl from the land of Israel. He demonstrated that the unity and co-laboring of women regardless of the diversity of the generational divide, social, economic, and hierarchy status, etc., much can be achieved.

2 Kings 5:1 Now Naaman, commander of the army of the king of Syria, was a great and honorable man in the eyes of his master because by him the Lord had given victory to Syria. He was also a mighty man of valor, but a leper.

In this story, the two people God engaged to spearhead Naaman's healing, was the maidservant, and her mistress.

5:2 And the Syrians had gone out on raids and had brought back captive a young girl from the land of Israel. She waited on Naaman's wife.

Being taken captive and removed from her land was a traumatic and terrifying experience for the young girl. Leaving behind family, friends, community, and familiar surroundings and being taken to the unknown could have had a devastating effect on her.

But, when one is rooted and grounded in their God, they know He will do mighty exploits in and through them. Born again, believers do not dwell in a captive mentality or any negative state. For Naaman, an unbeliever to know about Elisha, God engaged a young girl who knew about the God of Israel. She became the bearer of good news and proclaimer of His signs and miracles to the household of Naaman.

You may ponder on why distress, discomfort, sufferings, or the injustices of life to cross your path. Whether these misfortunes are self-inflicted, or the enemy's afflictions or God orchestrated, are, to a certain degree, inconsequential. What matters is your trust in God. Without a doubt, He will turn these unfortunate happenings for your good and will cause them to work in your favor.

Promotion and good treatment for the young captive were inevitable after Naaman's healing. Besides, she was sure to find favor because she was the messenger and deliverer of good news. Wallow in self-pity was not an option because she was a captive. Neither was she silent about her God because of the situation she found herself in. She spoke out and proclaimed the good news and the wonder-working power of the God of Israel. Bold amid her captors, she spoke of the power of her God. She had fallen into a dire situation but did not pay heed to what her captors would think. Agonizing thoughts could have plagued her mind. If her God was so mighty to heal, was able to set captives bound by infirmities free, why hadn't He set her free? Why was she in a dreadful situation? Why had He allowed her to be captured and why had He not rescued her?

5:2 And the Syrians had gone out on raids and had brought back captive a young girl from the land of Israel. She waited on Naaman's wife.

The young girl waited on Naaman's wife. She was not prideful, knowing she was an Israelite, the chosen one of God (Ammo Israel). Being in the services of a non-believer did not diminish her identity on who she was. Embedded in her was the assurance of knowing that she was the head and not the tail, above and not beneath, the daughter of the Most High God. Just as Naaman waited faithfully on his master, she too waited faithfully on her mistress. God gave her the boldness to speak to her mistress, and she said;

5:3 *"If only my master were with the prophet who is in Samaria. For he would heal him of his leprosy.*

Because she seemed to be the least likely to be used by God, considering her situation, it did not stop her from speaking out. Neither did she dwell on the fact that defeated by the Syrians, so nothing good would come out of Samaria.

Unfortunate or unfavorable situations that you may find yourself in, or the misconceived belief that nothing good can come out of you, your family, community, or nation, are not based on God's truth. It is not where you are at, the historical background, or the geographical location you come from that determines your destiny, but the seed of purpose God has placed in the inside of you. When He deems it's the right germinating season, He releases and utilizes it. It was not the situation that the young Israelite found herself in, but what she had on the inside of her. When it came to full maturity God released it, and she was able to speak out boldly about Naaman's leprosy. With her God-given ability, she was able to discern and sense that it plagued and tormented him. God, in His unlimited ways, demonstrated His power and strategy as a revealer of secrets. Perhaps He allowed her to overhear Naaman speak to his wife about his condition. Or God prompted the wife to speak to her about her husband's leprosy. But whatever the occurrences were that opened the door, she used the opportunity to speak out. She was bold and obedient in approaching her mistress about her master's leprosy.

The God-given authority and opportunity for 'born again' believers to be bold in addressing negative, harmful situations or conduct. God's healing, saving grace, and compassion, etc. are manifest through this boldness. With the wisdom of God and guidance of the Holy Spirit, we may boldly confront issues without eluding the discomfiting, awkward, or the complexity of the situation.

The second person, God, engaged in Naaman's healing was his wife. Had she been an uncaring, disobedient, and selfish wife instead of a helpmate, she could have shunned, ignored, or dismissed the young girl's advice. Pride, arrogance, and an inflated self-importance attitude could have been a stumbling block because of the difference in their social status. The possibilities of Naaman's wife rejecting her maidservant's advice were astronomical. Not only was she young, inexperienced in giving advice, but it was not her place to give Godly counsel or suggestions. Her primary duty was to wait on her and to perform her chores. But the wife harkened to her maidservant's voice, which led to her husband's healing.

The maxim that 'behind every successful man/woman is a good woman/man' stands true and fast to this day. She wanted and cared for his wellbeing and the success of her household. The success of a nucleus family, household, community, etc. is dependent on the mutual respect of husbands/wives, mothers/fathers, children, etc. especially those in the household of God.

The two people who did not participate in Naaman's healing were the two kings, the king of Syria and the king of Israel. The king of Syria had the misconception that his money and gifts could buy Naaman's healing for he said;

5:5 Then the king of Syria said, "Go now, and I will send a letter to the king of Israel. So he departed and took with him ten talents of silver, six thousand shekels of gold, and ten changes of clothing.

Because of Naaman's great victories for the king and his country, he found favor with the king. Hence the king did not hesitate to write the letter, giving him money and sending him off to Israel with these gifts. But Naaman's healing was not in the gifts and money.

The weight of this evidence indicates that our trust should not be on monetary value or material possessions. These very treasures can be to our detriment, as in the case of Gehazi's greed, Elisha's servant. (Read 1 Kings 5:20-27).

The king of Israel found himself also in a real dilemma. As a responsible leader and ruler over his subjects, he was expected to have a solution for his people. The same responsibility lies with the 21st-century rulers. Together with the cabinet ministers whom they surround themselves with, they are expected to have solutions for the crisis that assail their countries. If people are unable to resolve complex social, economic issues, etc., these catastrophes compel them to gravitate towards the government seeking intervention. But like Naaman, our healing, whether physical, psychological, and the many calamities that plague families, societies, and nations, is not found in kings, in leaders or government. Many answers to life's challenges are found on bended knees from the one true God who utilizes and releases potential, skills, talents, and gifts, etc. embedded within every individual.

The king of Israel cried out to his enemy, the king of Syria. As a true servant of the people connected to his people, he would have known about the servant of God, Elisha, in his land. But because of his spiritual ignorance and blindness, there was a disconnection. The king did he not have the wisdom to resolve what he perceived as a quarrel or the problem in his nation. He was also unaware of the power of God through His servant in his land,

Hosea 4:6 MY people are destroyed for lack of knowledge. Because you have rejected knowledge, I also will reject you from being priest for Me, because you have forgotten the law of your God, I also will forget your children.

Because of the lack of knowledge to serve and know God personally, leaders have also failed to recognize the existence of the true servants' of God in their nations. A majority of heads of states did not know about the power of God through His servants. In their short-sightedness and ignorance, they have also rejected the wisdom of God as a partner in the affairs of their nations. As priests unto God and true shepherds, rulers should be able to access direction, guidance, and divine intervention to leads His sheep. The price of rejection paid by the people in the land as God says, *'I also will forget your children.'*

These rulers are spiritually cut-off from God's wisdom, understanding, and empathy for their people. Many have insatiable greed. Many manipulated in engaging in evil deeds by foreign interventions, whether spiritual or literal. Some govern with constant disruption to their rule by terrorism and insurgents supported by foreign multinational and political aid, etc. All these onerous conflicts ravish at their inner peace and undermine their ability to govern their nations decisively and effectively. However, in recent times, the servants of God have made themselves known to their governments. Some have made themselves known aggressively, unashamedly, and with no compromise. King Jesus Lord and Saviour, when represented in a household, a family, a community, and a nation, gives one the boldness and the provision to fulfill one's calling.

5:8 So it was when Elisha the man of God heard that the king of Israel had torn his clothes, that he sent to the king, saying, "Why have you torn your clothes? Please let him come to me, and he shall know that there is a prophet in Israel."

In other words, Elisha was asking the king, why have you exposed your weaknesses and vulnerability? Why have you disarmed, disrobed, and stripped yourself of your rulership and authority? Some rulers have unashamedly exposed their weaknesses in their inability to govern their nations effectively. Unfortunately, this inability due to unacceptable behavior has crippled and stigmatized their nations and defamed their reputations.

Issues rulers are unable to resolve should be in the capable hands of God's people, 'please let them come to us.'

A government unable to meet the peoples' needs, compels them to find or to seek healing, provision, etc. in the house of God.

5:9 Then Naaman went with his horses and chariot, and he stood at the door of Elisha's house.

9

THE SPIRIT OF BOLDNESS

A RIGHTEOUS GIFT

The spirit of boldness is a source of power needed to help affect one's purpose in life. The Lord foreknew the conniving plots the enemy would use prohibiting you from fulfilling your purpose. In His mercy and grace, He formulated a plan against his wicked schemes deployed to shut you down. Some of the strategies would be through intimidation, the fear of man, internal and external strife in homes, relationship issues, communities, nations, etc. These are some of his blueprints designed to prevent the word of God through your purpose from being proclaimed.

The enemy who has come to steal, kill, and destroy (John 10:10) He is vicious in his attacks which are against the kingdom of God, His people, as stated in;

Matthew 11:12, "And from the days of John the Baptist, until now the kingdom of God suffers violence and the violent take it by force."

Hence God has equipped and empowered His kingdom army with the power of boldness to fight back. Like Jeremiah in reproach and derision and although mocked daily, was undeterred;

Jeremiah 20: 8-9 But His word was in my bones like a burning fire, Shut up in my bones, I was weary of holding it back, and I could not.

God's passion imbued in Jeremiah to effect what God had called him to undertake, reproach and derision did not stop him. Therefore as long as God has a passion burning in your soul to effectuate His will, you should not hold back. In every born again believer, the word of God burns in their bones, waiting for release in utterance or action. Expressing boldness is not necessarily on a pulpit, or social media platforms, et. But it can be in a work environment, in the community, neighborhood, nursing homes, homeless shelters, etc. The list is endless, where the word of God can be released.

Defeat is inevitable if intimidated in the many forms, and appearances fear presents itself. Besides, a weak disposition, words of doubt, and unbelief from family, friends, or anyone will undermine your ability to accomplish your purpose. The re-surfacing of the past, guilt, wrong decisions, and choices, etc., may resonate to haunt you or count you unworthy or uncalled. These are some of the most pernicious stumbling blocks to the fulfillment of your purpose and destiny. But again God has not left you defenseless for He said in;

John 19:30b 'It is finished,' to the consternation of the naysayers as they watch your 'Arising' and your absolute belief in;

Romans 8:1 there is therefore now no condemnation to those who are in Christ Jesus and behold we are new creations.

2 Corinthians 5:17 Therefore, if anyone is in Christ, he is a new creation, old things have passed away, behold all things have become new, the old man has died.

Not only are we to be bold in action but in speaking the word and proclaiming Christ;

2 Corinthians 11:21 says I speak as concerning reproach, as though we had been weak. But in whatever anyone is bold, I speak foolishly; I am bold also.

Philippians 1:14 says; And most of the brethren in the Lord, having become confident by my chains, are much more bold to speak the word without fear.

Trials and tribulations should not hinder you nor cause you to retreat in shame, fear, guilt, etc. but to speak of the gospel, which will, in turn, encourage others to be bold. It is only the understanding of the truth embedded in the gospel that sets us free. But if misunderstood or misconstrued, it may appear to be a mystery.

Ephesians 6:19-20 And for me, that utterance may be given to me, that I may open my mouth boldly to make known the mystery of the gospel. For which I am an ambassador in chains; that in it, I may speak boldly, as I ought to speak.

Where do you go in times of need without fear of receiving this boldness? A visible shaking of your faith by a myriad of complexities. Where do you go? Depressive thoughts. Where do you go when utter darkness congests your mind, or in moments of weakness and anxious uncertainties bring you to the brink of collapse?

Hebrews 4:16 says, *Let us, therefore, come boldly to the throne room of grace, that we may obtain mercy and find grace to help in time of need.*

And we may boldly say,

Hebrews 13:6 "The Lord is my helper; I will not fear. What can man do to me?

In times of calamity, when joyful or in times of persecution, you can boldly proclaim *the Lord, my helper in every aspect.*

The confidence to have boldness is through Christ and an indivisible faith in Him.

Ephesians 3:12 In Him, we have boldness and access with confidence by the faith of Him.

Philippians 1:20 According to my earnest expectation and my hope, that in nothing I shall be ashamed, but that with all boldness, as always, so now also Christ shall be magnified in my body, whether it be by life or by death.

Boldness in Christ is boldness in the highest dimension. This boldness, in most cases, comes with a price tag of service, i.e., having served as Naaman faithfully served.

- The price tag in the 21st century is the assurance of knowing Jesus loves you incomparably to other women to the extent that He gave His life for you. (Belief in called and chosen).

- A sacred fire that cannot be extinguished burns in your soul. He ensures it's not extinguished — fulfillment of your purpose.

- Pursuing you to step out and to step forward as a woman who will restore civil liberty in every area of humanity. (Defeats doubt).

1 Timothy 3:13 For they have used the office of a deacon well purchase to themselves a good degree, and great boldness in the faith which is in Christ Jesus.

Appropriating the boldness with the blood of Jesus, we confidently enter the Holy of Holies, the throne room of grace.

Hebrews 10:19 Having, therefore, brethren, boldness to enter into the holiest by the Blood of Jesus.

More of God's love infused and perfected in you when acts of boldness incorporated simultaneously with empathy and kindness. In the day of judgment boldness of Christ still reflected in you while still in the world

1 John 4:17 Herein is our love made perfect, that we may have boldness in the day of judgment: because as He is, so are we in this world.

DESTINY DESTROYERS

5:11 But Naaman became furious, and went away and said, Indeed I said to myself, He will surely come to me, and stand and call on the name of the Lord his God, and wave his hand over the place, and heal the leprosy.

Pride, the false notion and reliance on a superiority attitude terminates what could be a triumphant outcome as a breakthrough can come from the least likely place or person;

Philippians 2:3 Let nothing be done through selfish ambition or conceit, but in lowliness of mind let each esteem others better than himself/herself.

When 'born' again, God has given us the power to behave and to think in a morally upright way and to surrender to the Spirit. We have the liberty and the right to enjoy this freedom without restrictions placed upon us through arrogance, or esteeming oneself better than the downtrodden and weak. These sinful behaviors and sometimes burdensome situations can be brought on by our past errors or undesirable present circumstances. Jesus purchased our freedom with His Blood so that we did not entangle ourselves in the burdens of the flesh. To maintain this liberty without misusing it is by continually and faithfully acknowledging the One who has bequeathed it to us.

Before we were 'born again,' we had yokes of sin around our necks that oppressed and depressed us. This yoke weighs us down, always involving self, or one or more people. If not on self, then this yoke is laid on one's shoulders by two or more people who pull it together in unison. But when 'born again' we stand alone, accountable for our sins, therefore;

Philippians 2:12 states, Work out your own salvation with fear and trembling.

Once 'born again,' one is accountable for one's actions and position in Christ unless the affliction is an external influence beyond one's control. However, a yoke of bondage needs no longer be a contraption used over one's shoulders, i.e., a physical constraint, e.g., shackles or prison walls. Instead, these can also be strong psychological forces of emotional sentiments. These negative forces invade our minds when we are in a position of weakness, compromise, or in a desperate situation. Our strength fails when we are unable to stand fast when caught in a destructive downward spiral. Inability to resist the works of the flesh, and yielding to its desires will consume us. Internal or external issues of contention, if not dealt with decisively, will ultimately overwhelm us. Surrendering to these hostile pressures entangle us once again in a yoke of bondage. A counter-attack is to feed on the truth and the positivity of God's word and to fellowship with other saints in the Body of Christ. 'Born again' is a first-person experience and encounter with the intensity of the love of Christ. This is also a self-awakening of being in love with Jesus. A constant feed on the word on a daily or regular basis is essential once we acknowledge the agape love of God. Freedom in Christ nurtured and not taken for granted. When we have heard the word of encouragement the word that builds, we gravitate towards maturation;

Acts 20:32 So now, brethren, I commend you to God and to His grace, which is able to build you up and give you an inheritance among all those who are sanctified.

Philippians 2:14-15 I press towards the goal for the prize of the upward call of God in Christ Jesus. Therefore let us, as many as are mature, have this mind, and if in anything you think otherwise, God will reveal even this to you.

We have been sanctified to do the work that was predestined, and if unknown, to pray God reveals it to us;

Ephesians 2:10 For we are His workmanship, created in Christ Jesus for good works, which God prepared beforehand, which we should walk in them.

With the spirit of boldness, we can go into the throne room of grace, receive our inheritance, and accomplish God's purpose for our lives.

Hebrews 4:2 For indeed the gospel was preached to us as well as to them, but the word which they heard did not profit them, not being mixed with faith.

To step out and to reach one's destiny is to mix what we have heard, what we believe, and what we have to achieve in the kingdom of God with faith. Without faith, not only is it impossible to please God, but it is impossible to reach your God-ordained destiny.

Hebrews 11:6 But without faith, it is impossible to please Him, for he who comes to God must believe that He is and that He is a rewarder of those who diligently seek Him.

We may speak of faith that can move mountains, but if this faith is unable to remove mountains that have the façade of being insurmountable in our families, societies, and nations, then it's weak. God will reward our faith with a comfortable seat in the church pews, or one of conformity in the destructive ideologies of the world's systems.

10

CROSSING OVER

STEPPING OUT AND STEPPING IN

BOTH LITERALLY AND SPIRITUALLY TO FULFILL GOD'S MANDATE

In Deuteronomy 11:1-32, Moses spoke to the remnant who survived the wilderness and were about to cross the Jordan into the promised land. He forewarns the remnant that He was not speaking to their children who did not know nor had seen the chastening of the Lord. The children were oblivious to His mighty hand, His outstretched arm, and of the Lord's greatness. They could not testify to the signs and wonders He had performed on behalf of their parents in Egypt. They had not witnessed the miraculous crossing of the Red Sea, the drowning, and the destruction of Pharoah and his great army. The torpedoing of their horses and chariots. Nor had they seen the punishment of the rebellion of Dathan and Abiram and their households. Neither could they attest to how the earth had opened its mouth and swallowed them up, their households, their tents, and all the substance that was in their possession. Moses said the Lord was speaking specifically to the parents. He reiterates that as parents, the onus was upon them to pass the history onto their children and the generations to follow. As their eyes had seen every great act of the Lord that He had done, it was their responsibility to relay this narrative.

Since the inception of the manuscript of the bible, nothing has detracted from the fact that there is a truth to be communicated. This biblical narrative structure is grounded in the very existence of humankind. However, man's continuance to exist in a life covered in a measure of prosperity, peace, and harmony is dependent on his obedience to God's word. But regardless of how God's word has been disseminated or communicated, obeyed, or disobeyed, the consistent central message in the bible is evident that God desires to have a personal relationship with each generation. Therefore to keep this narrative relevant and alive is to pass the message effectively. An effective way is by manifesting and proclaiming the goodness of God in the acts He has performed and continues to perform in our lives. The miracles found in the Old and New Testament are undeniably evident in our lives today. Keeping God current, relevant, and His interaction with humanity alive is of the utmost importance and not distant from our everyday livelihood, events, and issues that pertain to life. Relevancy also points to the sole belief that the signs and wonders He performed in the Old Testament were going to be emulated in the Word made flesh, Jesus the Messiah. God had prepared a solid foundation in the Old Testament for the belief in His Son Jesus. He was confident that Jesus would do the same through those who believed and accepted Him as the Son of God. Jesus kept the Father and his kingdom alive. He emulated the characteristics of the Father in the signs and wonders He performed and by way of storytelling, i.e., teaching in parables. Therefore God holds every generation accountable to keep the word alive and active. Each generation is to pass the historical and the current mighty acts, signs, and wonders of God functional and operational. The demonstration of the word in the miracles He continues to execute daily on our behalf as our Father. He does this through His sons and daughters, who are in Christ Jesus, the Anointed One, His Begotten Son.

The word of the Lord is relevant and applicable to the current generation as it was to the ancient Israelites. God is now speaking to the current generation who have journeyed through the storms of life and have survived. This generation has crossed over into the new season and is about to enter the promises of God. God commanded the Israelites, and said, 'Keep my commandments. He is commanding us now and saying, "Keep my word, and you will be strong enough to go in and to possess the land," i.e., your vision, dream, or goal so that you may live long enough to see its fruition.

STEPPING OUT AND STEPPING IN

The illustration of the following verses as they applied to the Israelites then relates and applies to those who wish to enter into their promised land, i.e., a God-given vision, dream, or goal.

11:10 For the land which you enter to possess is not like the land of Egypt from which you have come, where you sowed your seed and watered it by foot, as a vegetable garden.

In the accomplishment of the purpose, nothing compares to what awaits as you step out and step in. Confronting unpleasant pasts, obstacles, and laborious toiling, etc., is immeasurable to what is to be released in and through you as you cross over to take possession of your vision, dream, goal, etc.

11:11 But the land which you cross to possess is a land of hills and valleys, which drinks water from the rain of heaven.

The land (vision, dream, goal)has its challenges to maintain (fulfill) but also has an overflow of abundant blessings.

For the fulfillment of purpose, God has an enabling plan for a fearless transition to assist in the cross over. Awaiting is divine heavenly help, i.e., wisdom, anointing, and provision that will be available for the fulfillment and to propel you forward.

11:12 A land for which the Lord your God cares, the eyes of the Lord your God are always on it, from the beginning of the year to the very end of the year.

The heavenly assistance is not only for the fulfillment of purpose but also as an indication that God cares for the vision, dream, or goal He has placed in you. Because He cares and loves the people whom He has set aside for you to impact, and to serve, etc. through the vision, dream, or goal, His eyes are always on them. His watchful eye hovers over them since the inception of creation and will continue beyond. His end of the year could be the coming of Christ, for God wants no man to perish.

11:13 And it shall be if you earnestly obey My commandments which I command you today, to love your God and serve Him with all your heart and with all your soul.

All God requires is obedience to His word, to love Him and to serve Him. Partaking of the abundant spiritual and natural blessings is also determined in wholehearted obedience.

To love God and to serve Him with all our heart and with all our soul, is through loving and serving one another.

Galatians 5:13 For you, brethren, have been called to liberty; only do not use liberty as an opportunity for the flesh, but through love serve one another.

Matthew 20:28 Just as the Son of Man did not come to be served, but to serve,

We serve God with our whole heart and strength. The heart is the dwelling place of the Lord's. He reciprocates our obedience and willing hearts to accommodate Him by filling us with a desire and a love to unselfishly serve one another and to count it all joy in meaningful gestures.

1 John 4:12 No one has seen God at any time. If we love one another, God abides in us, and His love has been perfected in us.

1 John 4:20 If someone says, 'I love God,' and hates his brother, he is a liar; for he who does not love his brother whom he has seen, how can he love God whom he has not seen?

Having chosen us, the Spirit of the Living God abides in our hearts. As an embodiment of love, He expects us to love one another. In-built spiritual tools are in humans equipping them to love. These spiritual tools help develop an intimate relationship with God that enables us to love one another. This intimate relationship enables us to dwell with Him and to love Him under the Blood of Jesus. Amplified and confirmation of His love in the word. Fellowship with other believers empowered through prayer, meditation, praise, and worship. Numerous other products are available for our spiritual growth, e.g., the Christian Arts and Culture Industry, i.e., Christian literature, movies, music, social gatherings, and celebrations, etc. These are all tools designed to strengthen our relationship with God and to help us mature in the knowledge and attributes of who He is.

We serve Him with our strength, if possible, by being physically involved in serving His people in community development and outreach programs. Participation in meaningful activities, as well as biblical teachings in the equipping of the saints and being ambassadors of Christ, is serving. Serving is also the presentation of tithes, offerings, evangelizing, and utilizing our material or other resources for the extension of God's kingdom.

11:14 Then I will give you the rain for your land in its season, the early rain and the latter rain, that you may gather in your grain, your new wine, and your oil.

There is a reciprocate blessing in serving and loving God in spiritual and practical ways. God will provide the early rain, i.e., fresh manna, revelation, and provision to sustain the (land) vision, dream, or goal. Assurance of relevance and fulfillment of the vision, dream, goal by the rain. Latter rain ensures the vision, and the visionary never runs dry. A season remains for what He has purposed to come to pass. Spiritual upliftment and growth in prayer, praise, worship, etc. are the tools that keep feeding the vision, dream, goal. Keeping the vision alive is the Lord's assurance that you, as the visionary, do not run out of the provision. The provision is provided materially, financially, inclusive of mental and emotional support.

The prerequisite conditions, if met in verse 11:13, are the Lord's promises. The promises are released so that you may **gather** in your grain–to make fresh bread. Fresh revelation is what you have previously sown; you will reap, will not be lost. Fresh revelation enables you to make fresh bread, i.e., to receive a 'now' word, a relevant word, a word that the Lord has not revealed before. These are secret treasures of heaven not yet released in the earth. Also, the gathering will be the ushering in of new souls, uncompromising believers ready to do the will of God. These are men and women, boys and girls, whom God has chosen to receive His word released through you.

The **New wine** is the Rhema word of God's, which is the prophetic utterance of the Holy Spirit, declaring He will pour out His Holy Spirit so that He is encountered and experienced in new ways. God will pour His new wine into new wineskins, i.e., new believers. These are people who are hungry and thirsty for Him. New wine is new teachings and new ways of doing church. The outpouring of the new wine is to serve Him excellently, love Him unconditionally, worship Him in spirit and truth, praise unreservedly and unashamedly, and pray fervently in new ways, etc.

The Old Testament teachings on being filled with the Holy Spirit, as found in Amos 9:13, confirm the in-pouring of new believers. What has been sown in the natural is superseded by spirit by the power of God and the New Testament teachings on being filled with the Holy Spirit as found in;

Ephesians 5:18 And do not be drunk with wine, in which is dissipation; but be filled with the Holy Spirit.

and *Acts 2:13 Others mocking said,' They are full of new wine.'*

This new move of God is that the in-pouring of new believers will not be drunk with intoxicating wine. They will no longer be filled with intoxicating wine but will be filled with the Holy Spirit, confirming a non-compromise of God's word. It does not change nor accommodate the ever-changing climate nor the ever-shifting paradigms of the 21-century dynamics.

A call to repentance:

Joel 2:12-13b Now, therefore, says the Lord,' Turn to Me with all your heart. With fasting, with weeping, and mourning.' So rend your hearts, not your garments.

And *Deuteronomy 33:28 Israel shall dwell in safety. The fountain in Jacob alone, in a land of grain and new wine. His heavens shall also drop dew.*

As hearts are rendered and in humble repentance turn to God, there'll be a time of refreshing, blessings of favor, and fulfillment of God's promises as the end-time harvest of souls come into His Kingdom.

There's a shift in communities, nations, and the global church, as people's lives are changed. There is an ushering in and an abundant outpouring of signs and wonders through the Body of Christ in the end-time harvest.

The rain also brings a change not only in the natural consumption needs for man, animals, and nature, etc. but also in the spiritual atmosphere as a sign of the outpouring of the Holy Spirit. (Read Acts 1;8a, 2;17-18 and Joel 2; 23,28) Prior belief and the misconception is that if there's barren soil, the hardness of the ground, then the earth cannot produce. The same analogy applies to the spiritual. If there is a lack of rain that is fresh manna, the 'now' word, it causes apathy and even the hardening of hearts. There come resistance and opposition to stop the rain as it empowers, restores, refreshes, and brings dead things to life. But with God, nothing is impossible. In this season God says in;

Isaiah 43:19 Behold, I will do a new thing, now it shall spring forth, Shall you not know it? I will even make a road in the wilderness and rivers in the desert.

The move not to be missed by the people of God as God does new things individually, corporately, in nations, and the Body of Christ globally.

11:14 and your oil - Psalm 92:10b I have been anointed with fresh oil and your oil- open heaven comes with the anointing, the enabler, the teacher, sanctified with the power to do the work of the Lord's.

1 John 2:27 But the anointing which you have received from Him abides in you, and you do not need that anyone teaches you; but as the same anointing teaches you concerning all things, and is true, and is not a lie, and just as it has taught you, you will abide in Him.

The Holy Spirit is the enabler who teaches all things. He enables us to abide in Him, to love Him, to serve Him, to love one another, and to serve one another. The love is drawing all men unto Him.

Psalm 133:1-2 Behold how good and how pleasant it is when brethren dwell together in unity! It is like the precious oil upon the head, running down on the beard, The beard of Aaron, Running down on the edge of his garments.

The precious oil, anointing, wisdom, and favor of God upon the head, flowing from a mind of Christ in you, the enabler who regardless of race, tribe, nation. Tongue and creed, cause brethren to dwell together in harmony.

11:15 And I will send grass in your fields for your livestock, that you may eat and be filled.

An abundance of the good things of God, more love, and there is no lack of nutritional and spiritual provision as well as resources for God's people.

Your field, your livestock, i.e., the people, congregations, communities, will be healthier spiritually, mentally, physically, and emotionally. There's a surplus of nourishment for the body, spirit, and soul. Spiritual satisfaction and the physical manifestation of fulfillment of your purpose supersedes the natural ingestion.

Man cannot lay claim to what God is doing. Only God will give you favor in your field of expertise, specialty, or in the simplicity of the occupation of your calling. The project or assignment will surely be beneficial to the kingdom of God, and you will reap the reward apportioned to you. Being bold, you will eat and are satisfied. As *man cannot live on bread alone, but by every word that proceeds from the mouth of God, Matthew 4:4* the eating and filling will be of spiritual satisfaction.

11:16 Take heed to yourself lest your heart be deceived, and you turn aside and serve other gods and worship them.

We must beware of immaturity, jealousy, competitiveness, and spiritual covetousness. We must guard our spiritual growth, lest our hearts deceive us;

The lust of the eye, the lust of the flesh and the pride of life 1 John 2:16

Serving other gods—a trap of material possessions, the ideologies of the systems of the world, or when unequally yoked, cause you to worship other gods. An example is Solomon, who served his wives, many gods. Or we may turn from the reverential fear of God to fear man, e.g., Elijah flees from Jezebel. Intimidated we may put our trust in man, e.g., Saul's turning away from trusting God and putting his trust in a medium of another spirit.

11:17 Lest the Lord's anger be aroused against you, and He shut up the heavens so that there be no rain, and the land yield no produce, and you perish quickly from the good land which the Lord is giving you.

Fresh revelation or growth in any area ceases as heaven's shut. There's no vision, or if there is, it does not materialize or come to fruition, and purpose remains unfulfilled, etc. You perish quickly, with no personal or spiritual growth. Negative influences of the land overcome you. These consume you and cause you to compromise. Unavoidable is the fact that in each land, there are giants to overcome who resist change and resist the word of God. They resist the positive spiritual influence and are resistive even to the spiritual shift that's tangible in the atmosphere. (spiritual giants-can be manifest in and through humanity or the dark cloud that hangs over God's people shutting their eyes and ears to hear the word of God - the prince of the kingdom of Persia – read Daniel 10:13-14)

11:22 Be careful to obey all the commands I give you, show love to the Lord your God by walking in His ways and clinging to Him.

Obedience is not only applicable to the spiritual realm. Obedience applied in every area of one's life, e.g., honoring an employment contract, ministry calling, etc. to reap the natural benefits of the company. The same principles apply in the spiritual sphere; obedience to God's word has an abundance of supernatural blessings, which are also manifest in the natural realm.

11:23 Then the Lord will drive out all these nations from before you, then you will dispossess greater and mightier nations than yourselves.

Gaining God's favor, His wrath averted and directed at the enemy is through obedience.

God will remove obstacles, even people who come against the fulfillment of a God-ordained purpose. No obstacles or challenges will be an impossibility to overcome. You overcome by the blood of the Lamb and the word of your testimony. In all things, you can overcome to accomplishment through Him who gives you strength.

11:24 Every place on which the sole of your foot treads shall be yours.

God will open doors to possess your vision, dream, goal that no man can open and will shut those prohibiting you from fulfilling your purpose.

WOMEN – GOD'S ARTISANS

Exodus 25:2,8 says; Then the Lord spoke to Moses saying: 'Speak to the children of Israel, that they bring Me an offering. From everyone who gives with a willing heart, you shall take My offering.

"And let them make Me a sanctuary, that I may live among them.

The Lord told Moses to make Him a tabernacle. He gave him specific furnishing instructions. The exact dimension and architectural design and construction.

And in turn, Moses told the children of Israel,

Exodus 35: 10 'All who are gifted artisans among you shall come and make what the Lord has commanded you.

The Lord provided Moses with men and women whom He had endowed with skills and gifts to help him build the Tabernacle.

The tabernacle furnishings constructed, each with its distinctive piece. In the house of God, each woman has a distinctive piece they are supposed to construct, i.e., a role to accomplish to complete the tabernacle, i.e., people of God. What piece has the Lord commanded you to make? What role has God instructed you to complete in your church, community, society, nation?

Exodus 35:25-26 All the women who were gifted artisans spun yarn with their hands, and brought what they had spun, of blue, purple and scarlet, and fine linen.

God has graciously placed a skill in the hand of each woman. The colors of the yarn they spun represent the special gifts. These skills wrought in and through the hands of women.

Blue signifying the Healing Power of God –

He said in *Mark 16:18b, 'you shall lay hands on the sick, and they shall be healed.*

It also represents depth, trust loyalty, sincerity, confidence, stability, faith, and intelligence, bringing peace and a sense of calmness in homes, communities, nations, etc. What internal qualities of God do we exhibit?

Purple associated with royalty, nobility, and power. Purple also represents wealth, wisdom, dignity, devotion, peace, and grandeur, confirming;

1 Peter 1:9a But you are a chosen generation, a royal priesthood, a holy nation, His own special people, that you may proclaim the praises of Him who called you out of darkness into His marvelous light.

We carry ourselves with a sense of pride and dignity, portraying royalty, and as priests unto God, proclaiming the good news. Able to bring light in the darkness. Confirming our faith that we believe we have been chosen, called, and delivered out of the darkness.

Scarlet a brilliant red color that evokes the color of blood and therefore symbolizes the Blood of Christ on the Cross. Red also symbolizes fire, the color of the Holy Spirit, action, confidence, and courage. But above all, the color red symbolizes the love of God represented through the sacrifice of Jesus Christ on the Cross.

Red in the days of old was also associated with immorality, particularly prostitution. But God in His mercy has delivered His daughters from the entanglements of the world to do His will. The Old Testament women prepared the way for the New Testament women to walk in the works God had prepared in advance. Empowered by His Holy Spirit, they can live uprightly and diligently and unselfishly give of the sacrificial love of God.

Exodus 35:29 The children of Israel brought a freewill offering to the Lord. All the men and women whose hearts were willing to bring material for all kinds of work which the Lord, by the hand of Moses, had commanded to be done.

Provided with everything when leaving Egypt, the Israelites understood it was from the Lord. When leaving Egypt, He commanded the Egyptians to give them their gold and silver. (Read Ex 11:2) When building the Tabernacle, they willingly brought what He had given them when they left Egypt. And there was material for all kinds of work which the Lord had commanded Moses to do. The tabernacle was constructed with specific specifications and a distinctive piece to furnish it in the inside.

So too, the Lord has equipped His daughters not only with spiritual skills but has allowed the accumulation of material possession and wealth, which are tools to be used in the construction of His Tabernacle. Of course, this is no longer just a physical construction, but also the spiritual construction of His people. A gift to be used in the construction of the lives of people, which enables God to live in and amongst them.

1 Corinthians 6:19 Or do you not know that your body is the temple of the Holy Spirit who is in you, whom you have from God, and you are not your own.

2 Ephesians 2:10 For we are His workmanship, created in Christ Jesus for good works for good works, which God prepared beforehand that we should walk in them.

Exodus 35:10 All who are gifted artisans among you shall come and make what the Lord has commanded you. The tabernacle (the people, community, nation) each with its distinctive piece – what piece are you supposed to construct, what piece has the Lord commanded you to make in your family, community, nation? A local or community program, a charity affiliation, or networking with one, supporting within your capability, spiritually, materially, financially, etc.

11

MARY MAGDALENE

THE FIRST – A PLAY

THE FIRST- RECIPIENT OF THE FIRSTFRUITS
LUKE 8:1-3 MATTHEW 27:55-61 MARK 16:1-10 JOHN 20:1-18

LUKE 8:1-3 'Now it came to pass, afterward, that He went through every city and village, preaching and bringing the glad tidings of the kingdom of God. And the twelve were with Him. And certain women who had been healed of evil spirits and infirmities – Mary called Magdalene, out of whom had come seven demons, and Joanna the wife of Chuza, Herod's steward, and Suzanna and many others who provided for Him from their substance.

SCENE ONE

Mary Magdalene asks Joanna the wife of Chuza if Jesus will stop at a certain village,
"Do you think Jesus will stop in this village?
Joanna, "I don't know, maybe He will, maybe He won't."
"What do you think, Suzanna?"
"He should. There is a great need there."
"Yes, I think He will stop. There's the sick, the hungry, the lame, the wayward."(The unemployed, the impoverished, the drug-dependent, etc.)
Mary Magdalene, "I want to set up my stall there to sell my goods. There's plenty I've already made, and I need to purchase more yarn."
Entering the village, Jesus approaches Mary Magdalene.
"Mary, you can sell your goods in the village. I will be teaching and bringing the glad tidings of the kingdom of God here."

Mary Magdalene, out of whom He had cast out seven demons, bows her head and thanks, Jesus.

"Yes, my Lord, thank You, Rabboni."

Mary Magdalene ponders on Jesus' words. 'How did He know I wanted to do my business here?'

Joanna asks Mary Magdalene what Jesus had said to her.

"He said we would be stopping here," replies Mary Magdalene.

"The supplies are low, so this will bring a substantial amount to carry us through to the next village. Here we can also purchase more supplies.

"Okay, run along then. Suzanna helps Mary Magdalene to the village market. Help her set up her stall and come right back, and help me settle the twelve and the Master for a rest before He starts the next meeting," says Joanna.

Mary Magdalene, with the help of Suzanna, gathers her goods. She folds her wooden table made by Jesus, who had imparted the carpentry skill into His earthly father, Joseph. Mary Magdalene comments on its beauty.

"This is the most exquisite handcrafted work I've ever seen."

"It sure is," says Suzanna, also looking admiringly at the folding table.

Mary Magdalene picks up her basket full of her knitted products. In it is a range of baby goods shawls, blankets, booties, jerseys, bonnets, picnic blankets, small and large quilts. They bundle everything hurriedly and set off to the village market. On arrival, they begin to wager for the best and busiest spot.

"This will do," says Suzanna.

"This one is better," says Mary Magdalene moving towards a clean and busy spot.

Just then, the stall owner hurries over to them as they are about to set up their table and goods.

"Hey," he yells at them, "that's a prime spot, and it's twenty denari," he says.

"What?" says Mary Magdalene, "that's a rip-off."

"Take it or leave," says the stall owner.

"Here." Mary Magdalene pulls out a ten denari and places it into his outstretched hand, "Take it or leave it," she says and walks away.

The stall owner grunting and mumbling under his breath takes it, shoves it into his apron pocket, and walks away.

"How did you do that?" Suzanna asks in amazement.

"We are about the Master's business, and He has blessed the work of our hands. The world is full of crafty business people. Remember what the Master said?"

"What did He say," Suzanna asks.

Matthew 10:16 "Behold I send you out as sheep in the midst of wolves. Therefore be wise as serpents and harmless as doves." Mary Magdalene replies.

"Oh, yes," I remember. "And Jesus also said He would bless the work of our hands, and this vendor was trying to cheat us," she adds.

They quickly set up the stall displaying the goods attractively on the table.

Once she had finished helping Mary Magdalene, Suzanna prepares to go back. Mary Magdalene embraces her and sends her off. "Thank you, my sister," she whispers.

"The Lord is with you. See you later."

"And is with you too," Suzanna replies, turns, and walks away.

Immediately the young pregnant women of the village surround Mary Magdalene's stall and begin admiring and purchasing her goods. The crowd attracts more people, and within an hour, she is sold out.

While she is cashing up, short Zacchaeus, the little village rogue, watches her from a little distance away. Suddenly he runs up to her and snatches her money bag from the table.

"Hey, stop!" Mary Magdalene tries to grab him, but the little rascal gets away from her. Instead, he runs smack bang into Peter. Knowing she had finished and foreseeing the trouble she was about to get into, Jesus had sent Peter to pick her up.

"Oh no, you don't," Peter grabs young Zacchaeus by the scruff of his neck and snatches the money bag out of his hand.

"Away with you and be delivered," he says, shoving him away.

Zacchaeus almost falls as he scrambles upright and scurries away.

A little distance away, young Zacchaeus stops and ponders at Peter's words.

'Be delivered,' he keeps repeating the words over and over to himself until he gets to his home.

(Grown into a rich young man, one day he hears that Jesus would be passing through Jericho. Knowing Peter would be with Him and remembering his words, he decides to go. But he was unable to see Jesus for he was of short stature.) Read Luke 19:1-10

Peter walks over to Mary Magdalene who witnessed the entire scene and handed her the money bag.

"Thank you," she says. "How did you know? I mean, your timing was so perfect. How did you know I was finished selling?" she asks in astonishment.

"The Master knew trouble was lurking. Knowing you had finished your business, He sent me to collect you," Peter replies, picking up the empty basket and folding her table.

"Praise is to God," Mary Magdalene says, silently shaking her head as she follows Peter. She mulls over Peter's words, 'the Master knew.'

Walking through the other stalls on their way back, Mary Magdalene purchases more yarn, material, and cotton at markedly reduced prices. She also purchases goods for the disciples, Jesus, the women, and supplies that she knows the ministry needs.

Luke 8:3b And Joanna of the wife of Chuza, Herod's steward and Susanna, and many others who provided for Him from their substance. Once more her basket full, they resume their journey back to join the others.

Arriving at their quarters, Mary Magdalene finds Jesus and the disciples have rested, have been fed, and are getting ready to go to the outskirts of the village where Jesus will be teaching. Immediately Mary Magdalene sets her goods down and gets ready to go with Jesus and the disciples.

"Are you not going to rest and have something to eat," Joanna and Suzanna ask.

"No, no, no time," Mary Magdalene replies.

Joanna quickly wraps a sandwich and pours some tea in a flask. She hands it to Suzanna to give it to Mary Magdalene, who had rushed out the door to follow Jesus and the disciples.

"Here," Suzanna places the package in her hand when she catches up with her.

"Thank you, my sister." Mary Magdalene quickly embraces her and runs off to catch up with Jesus and the disciples. She weaves her way through the crowd that had already gathered to follow Jesus. She puts the lunch package in a side pocket in the basket that has her work material. When Jesus finds a suitable spot, He tells the disciples to make the multitude to sit down. Mary Magdalene pulls out one of her best quilts. She lays it on the ground for Jesus to sit on. She lays a couple more for the disciples and a small one for herself. She sits at Jesus' feet, and the people sit on the grass as He begins to teach them. While Jesus teaches, Mary Magdalene sits knitting and tries to pay attention to what He is saying. Suddenly her mind starts to wander. She stops knitting and begins to reminisce about how Jesus delivered her from the seven demons. Jesus knowing that she is thinking of her past, lays His hand on her head.

"Mary, you are delivered. Behold old things have passed away, you are now a new creation."

"Mary immediately repents. "I'm sorry, Rabboni," murmurs, thank you and continues to knit.

While Jesus teaches, she grabs hold of the word and likens her situation to the seed. (Read Matthew 13:19-22) She begins to listen with her spiritual ears. Soon she starts to bear fruit of what she has learned. After teaching the multitude, and they had departed, she approaches Jesus.

"Master," she calls out.

"Yes, Mary." Jesus stops to listen to her.

"I'll make sure the seed You have sown in my heart is not trampled upon, devoured by the birds of the air or falls on rocks. I will not allow it to wither away, choked because of lack of moisture, nor fall among thorns. The revelations of mysteries of the kingdom of God I'll ensure fall on good ground.

Matthew 13:23 *"But he who received seed on good ground is he who hears the word and understands it, who indeed bears fruit and produces some a hundredfold, some sixty, and some thirty.*

And Jesus said to her, "To whom much is given much is required. Remember this, too, Mary."

Mary Magdalene made sure what she heard and what Jesus had done for her stayed in her heart, and was saved for her salvation. She resisted temptation and was not tempted to go back to her past. She ensured once she was set free, she did not revert to the snares of the world. Instead, she kept her mind blemish and stain free. She endeavored to keep her heart good and noble. With patience, she waited, knowing she was going to bear more good fruit. She understood that light had shone in her mind after darkness had previously occupied it. Concluding what's lit in her would not stay hidden or covered. She had to set it on a lampstand. She decided that those she interacted with, had to see her light, the Light of Jesus within her. She earnestly prayed they would be saved and would enter the kingdom of God.

While the disciples wanted to know why Jesus spoke to the multitude in parables;

Matthew 13:10 *'And the disciples came and said to Him," Why do You speak to them in parables?"*

"And Jesus said, "Because it has been given to you to know the mysteries of the kingdom of heaven, but to them, it has not been given."

Mary Magdalene wanted to know what the secret things of heaven were.

Jesus leans towards Mary Magdalene and says to her, "Mary, you seek the things of above which are eternal and not things of the earth He revealed the secrets to her.

Luke 8:17, *"For nothing is secret that will not be revealed, nor anything hidden that will not be made known and come to light."*

"Yes, Master," Mary Magdalene answers and smiles knowingly as the other disciples glare at her. And Mary Magdalene concealed all these things and pondered them in her heart.

Mary Magdalene understood the revealing of the secrets of Heaven. What the natural eye could not see then, would be made known to her in due course. Walking in the spirit with Jesus, she witnesses the revelation of more secrets.

Matthew 8:18 "Therefore take heed how you hear. For whoever has, to him more will be given, and whoever does not have, even what he seems to have will be taken from him."

She took heed of what He said, taught them, and understood that more would be given and revealed to her.

SCENE TWO

Then one day, Mary Magdalene's natural world was shattered. All she had kept in her heart began to unfold, and she remembered Jesus' words;

John 14:18 "You have heard Me say to you, 'I am going away and coming back to you,' If you loved Me, you would rejoice because I said, 'I am going to the Father, for My Father is greater than I. And now I have told you before it comes, that when it does come to pass, you may believe."

It was late evening while praying in the garden at Brook Kidron, a detachment of troops and officers came bound and arrested Jesus. Judas had betrayed Him.

Mark 14:18 Now, as they sat and ate, Jesus said, "Assuredly, I say to you, one of you who eats with Me will betray Me.

Mary Magdalene was sitting and praying with the other women a little distance away from Jesus, and the disciples were praying. She is the first to see the troops and officers approach Jesus. She jumps up and runs towards them calling out as she runs;

"Rabboni, Rabboni, what is going on?"

But just before she reaches Jesus, she hears Him ask,

John 18: 4-6, "Whom are you seeking?'

They answered Him, "Jesus of Nazareth." Jesus said to them, *"I Am He."*

Now when He said, "I Am He," they drew back and fell to the *ground.*

As Mary Magdalene gets close, she hears Jesus's words. And witnesses the soldiers falling to the ground. But before she can get to Jesus, she is barred by one of the soldiers as he raises from the ground. He grabs her by the arm, stopping her from getting to Jesus. Just then she sees Judas stealthily walking away from the crowd, and she lunges towards him, screaming,

"You traitor, it's you." The soldiers encircle and pull her away before she gets to Judas.

Jesus approaches the soldiers restraining Mary.

John 18:8 "I have told you, I am He. Therefore if you seek Me, let these go their way.

Jesus walks by Mary Magdalene and says, *"Peace be still, My peace I leave with you."*

But instead, Mary Magdalene breaks down and begins to weep. They took Jesus away.

John 18:12 Then the detachment of troops and the captain and the officers of the Jews arrested Jesus and bound Him.

The disciples and the women follow the troops and Jesus. Jesus is led into the court and brought before the High priest, but they are not allowed to enter the court.

Mary Magdalene tries to squeeze her way through. The soldiers stop her. The next day Jesus is sentenced to be crucified. Mary Magdalene and the other women witness the crucifixion as they follow Him to Golgotha.

Matthew 27:45 "Now from the sixth hour until the ninth hour there was darkness over all the land. And suddenly, the earth shook."

Crucified on that great is the King of kings and Lord of lords. The earth shook, and humanity trembled. The historical moment at His death and the enigmatic; the difficulty to explain the shaking of the earth that accompanied the crucifixion was beyond man's

128

comprehension. The conspirators believed they had a justifiable reason for His crucifixion;

But *1 Corinthians 2:8 says, none of the rulers of this age knew; for had they known, they would not have crucified the Lord of glory.*

And they continue to crucify Him daily. They remove Him from every public arena, every privatized space, and institutionalized place, and they try to push Him into the recess of every human mind.
Jesus dies on the cross.

"What's happening," Suzanna asked in fright, clinging to Mary Magdalene when the earth began to shake.

And Mary Magdalene recollects the anointing ceremony in Bethany at the house of Simon, the leper.

Matthew 26:6-7, 12-13 "And when Jesus was in Bethany at the house of Simon the Leper, a woman came to Him having an alabaster flask of very costly fragrant oil, and she poured it on His head as He sat at the table.

Calmly while everybody around them scrambled for safety when the earth shook, Mary Magdalene turns to her and says,

"Do you remember the story about the woman who poured oil on the Master's head at the house of Simon the leper and the disciples were indignant?" Mary Magdalene asks Suzanna.

"Yes I've heard of that story, but that was before I followed the Master," replies Suzanna.

"That woman was me. The Master did not rebuke me, a sinner, and a woman touching Him. Instead, He rebuked the disciples, delivered me, set me free. I have never been the same. When the Master rebuked the disciples, He said,

Mark 14:8, "For in pouring this fragrant oil on My body, she did it for My burial.

And He also said,

Mark 14:9 "Assuredly, I say to you, wherever this gospel is preached in the whole world, what this woman has done will be told as a memorial to her."

"So you knew this was going to happen, then. Oh, Mary, I am so sorry," Suzanna says as the two women cling to each other crying.

"But He is not dead," Mary Magdalene says between sobs, "He'll be back." She begins to cry even harder.

"But He said it's finished." Suzanna believes she's consoling Mary.

"Do not say that," Mary Magdalene turns to her angrily. "He means sin will never rule over humankind again, and death has lost its sting. We need not be afraid of death anymore because, in Him, we will live forever."

Suzanna looks at Mary Magdalene, completely puzzled.

"Oh no! you don't understand?" Mary Magdalene turns and looks away.

"I'm sorry…"

But Suzanna is cut short as Mary Magdalene interrupts her in mid-sentence. She puts a finger to her lips and whispers,

"Shhh."

They hear singing, the sound of angelic voices coming from where Jesus hangs on the cross.

Looking up, they see two people coming from either side of the cross, followed by two groups of people dressed in raggedy clothes. They bow before the cross singing;

'BEYOND THE CROSS.'

Before I found the Cross
I was confused and completely lost
The thought of death had me bound
My soul, I had sold for a pound
My spirit in sin drowned

Then I heard about the Cross
How He shed His Blood for me
I wondered and cried, how can that be
I have to go and see.

Then I looked at the Cross

There I found mercy and grace
Saw how He washed away my filth and dross
With His Blood washed away my shame and disgrace
With His Blood removed impurities within
 On the third day, He Arose
And all of hell but froze
Now I can gladly sing
O' death where is your sting
O' grave where's your victory
As I kneel and worship at His feet
I can proclaim my Redeemer lives
So too I shall surely live
Beyond the grave, my life goes on.

Then I saw the Cross,
Saw how He shed His Blood for me
I wondered and cried, how can that be
I had to go and see
And there I found mercy and grace
He whispered, your life's beyond the Cross.

Then right before their eyes, the raggedy clothes are transformed into beautiful white gowns.

"What did I tell you?" Mary Magdalene turns to Suzanna with a smile. "Sin will never rule over mankind again, and death has lost its sting."

Later, Mary mother of James and Joses joins Mary Magdalene and Suzanna.

Matthew 27: 55-56 And many women who followed Jesus from Galilee, ministering to Him, were there looking on from afar, among whom were Mary Magdalene, Mary the mother of James and Joses, and the mother of Zebedee's sons.

She remembers while walking with Him in, He said;

Luke 8:17 For nothing is secret that will not be revealed, nor anything hidden that will not be known and come to light. Therefore take heed how you hear, for whoever has, to him more will be given, and whoever does not have, even what he seems to have will be taken from him."

Matthew 27:57-58 Now when evening had come, there came a rich man from Arimathea, named Joseph, who himself had also become a disciple of Jesus. This man went to Pilate and asked for the body of Jesus.

Mary Magdalene and the other Mary rushed over to Him. They want to know about his trip and if Pilate had granted his request.

"What did Pilate say?' they ask Joseph.

"He has commanded Jesus' Body be given to us," Joseph replied.

Matthew 27:60 When Joseph had taken the body, he wrapped it in a clean linen cloth. And he laid it in his new tomb which he had hewn out of rock, and he rolled a large stone against the door of the tomb and departed.

"Why don't you go home now, the evening has come," Joseph says to the two Marys.

"We'll be fine, you go on," Mary Magdalene says to Joseph.

Matthew 27:61 And Mary Magdalene was there, and the other Mary, sitting opposite the tomb.

Mary, the mother of James and Joses, said to Mary Magdalene.

"It's been a long day, why don't you go and rest, the evening has come."

And Mary Magdalene replied and said," No, I can't leave Him now. He needs me now more than ever."

(Read Matthew 27:62-66)

When two soldiers came to guard the tomb, they found the two Marys still sitting opposite the tomb. Jeering and mocking them, they asked if they wanted to steal Jesus' body and then claim He had risen. One of the guards walks towards Mary Magdalene and ridicules her. He leans forward and leers in her face saying,

"Are you planning to steal His body and say to the people He has risen from the dead so that the last deception will be worse than the first, is that it?" he screams into her face. (Matthew 27:64b paraphrased)

"Away with you," Mary Magdalene says to the soldier. Rising from the stone she had been sitting on, she hastily gets onto her feet and forcefully pushes him away. The soldier stumbles backward. Straightening himself, he charges towards her. But the other soldier grabs him from behind and pulls him away.

"Get away from here," he shouts over the angry soldier's shoulder at Mary Magdalene and the other Mary.

"Come, let's go home. We can come back tomorrow," the other Mary pleads.

The two women walk away arm in arm.

Early the next morning,

Mark 16:1-2 Now when the Sabbath was past, Mary Magdalene, Mary, the mother of James and Salome bought spices, that they might come and anoint Him.

Early in the morning, Mary Magdalene is the first one awake and awakens the others.

"Come on, get up, it's time to get ready. We need to leave now," hastening Suzanna and Mary, the mother of James and Joses.

The women dress quickly and follow Mary Magdalene out the door, drawing their scarves over their heads.

Did you bring enough spices?" Mary, the mother of James, asked Mary Magdalene.

"Oh, yes. I want to make sure the Master even as He lies there. He smells of the sweet fragrance. What permeates from the tomb must not be the smell of death because He is not dead."

The other Mary and Suzanna look at each other and turn to look sympathetically at Mary Magdalene. They conclude she is in denial of Jesus' death.

So very early that morning, while everyone was still asleep, they left home. They walked quickly through the quiet and dark streets to the tomb. Heads and shoulders bowed down against the morning chill, they chatted speculating on what lay ahead. Mary Magdalene carried the basket full of spices on her arm.

Salome asked, "Who will roll away the stone from the door of the tomb for us?"

"Should we ask the soldiers guarding the tomb," she said.

But Mary mother of James said," maybe we should have asked Peter or James to come with us so they could help."

"Hope it's not the same soldiers," said Salome.

"Don't be afraid, they won't be there," said Mary Magdalene putting their minds at ease. "We will do it ourselves. The Master will give us strength. "

"But remember He is dead," said Salome," so how can He do that?

"Don't say that," Mary Magdalene snaps sharply, "He is not dead." As she speaks, she remembers Jesus' words that flash through her mind.

...and that He was buried and that He rose again on the third day.

Mary, the mother of James, comes alongside Mary Magdalene and puts a comforting arm around her shoulder. The threesome walk the rest of the way in silence. When they came to the tomb, the sun had risen.

Mark 16:4: But when they looked up, they saw that the stone had been rolled away for it was very large.

The rolled away stone is first seen by Mary Magdalene. Suddenly she thrust the basket into the other Mary's hand. Without saying a word, she gathers her skirts in her hands and breaks into a sprint leaving the other two women behind, exclaiming and crying out loud. They too break into a run when they realize what Mary Magdalene had seen.

"Oh no, no, no, don't let it be," Mary mother of James and Joses cries out. She drops the basket with the spices, and it's picked up by Salome, who was running behind her.

Mark 16:5 And entering the tomb, they saw a young man clothed in a long white robe sitting on the right side, and they were alarmed.

Mary mother of James and Salome cower behind Mary Magdalene who stood and asked,

"Who are you? What have you done with my Master, and where have you taken Him?'

Mark 16:6 But he said to them, "do not be alarmed, you seek Jesus of Nazareth, who was crucified, He has risen, He is not here...

"Yes, we have come to anoint Him, see the spices," says Mary Magdalene and reaches for the basket from Salome.

"He has risen, He is not here, see the place where they had laid Him," says the angel pointing to the place.

"Glory Hallelujah, I knew it, I knew it," says Mary Magdalene excitedly as she grabs the other Mary's hand and bolts out of the tomb.

"Hey," the angel calls after them before they reach the exit. They stop and look back at the angel.

Mark 16:7-8 "Go and tell His disciples and Peter that He is going before you into Galilee, there you will see Him as He said to you."

So they went out quickly and fled from the tomb.

"Hurry," says Mary Magdalene as she rushes out.

But Mary mother of James and Salome were slowing Mary Magdalene down, so she left them behind and ran ahead of them.

But before Mary Magdalene reaches the disciples, she suddenly stops. The smile erased from her face, and her countenance changes to sadness. 'But where in Galilee will we see Him,' she ponders aloud and then breaks into another run.

SCENE THREE

MARY MAGDALENE SEES THE RISEN LORD

Mark 16:9 Now when He rose on the first day of the week, He appeared first to Mary Magdalene, out of whom He had cast seven demons.

John 20:1-2 Now on the first day of the week, Mary Magdalene went to the tomb early, while it was still dark, and saw that the stone had been rolled away from the tomb. Then she ran and came to Simon Peter and to the other disciples, whom Jesus loved, and said to them. "They have taken away the Lord out of the tomb, and we do not know where they have laid Him.

Mary Magdalene outruns the others. She is the first to arrive and knocks loudly on the door where Simon Peter and the other disciples are staying.

"Whose there?" Simon Peter asks before opening the door.

"It's me," Mary Magdalene answers.

Simon Peter cautiously opens the door with one hand while wiping the sleep from his eyes with the other. He sees the stricken look on Mary Magdalene's face.

"What happened, where do you come from at this early hour of the morning? What's this racket about and why do you look like you've seen a ghost?" asked Simon Peter.

"They have taken the Lord out of the tomb, and we do not know where they have laid Him," says Mary Magdalene.

The other disciples walk over to the door and peer over Simon Peter's shoulder to see who he is talking too. Seeing it is Mary Magdalene, they push Simon Peter aside and pull her into the house and quickly bolted the door. The other disciples also ask Mary Magdalene what is going on.

And she said to them,

John 20:2b, "They have taken the Lord out of the tomb, and we do not know where they have laid Him."

"What do you mean we, who is we?" asks Peter.

"Mary mother of James and Salome who is with me," Mary Magdalene answers.

Then there's another knock, and one of the disciples goes to open the door and lets Mary mother of James and Salome, who had been following Mary Magdalene into the house.

"You stay here," Simon Peter says to the three women, "until we get back, we will go and see for ourselves."

"No, I'm not staying, I'm coming with you," says Mary Magdalene, and follows them out the house.

John 20:3 Peter, therefore, went out, and the other disciple were going to the tomb.

John 20:4: So they both ran together, and the other disciple outran Peter and came to the tomb first.

The other disciples outran Simon Peter because he had slowed down for Mary Magdalene's sake, who he could see was exhausted.

John 20:8 Then the other disciple, who came to the tomb first, went in also, and he saw and believed.

After they saw that the tomb was indeed empty and that Jesus' body was no longer there, only then did they believe her.

John 20:10 "Then the disciples went away again to their home.

"Are you coming," asks Simon Peter.

"No," replies Mary Magdalene.

John 20:11 But Mary Magdalene stood outside by the tomb weeping, and as she wept, she stooped down and looked into the tomb.

And at that moment, when she stooped down, it was more than a physical act. She was unknowingly performing a natural act that bound her to the spirit of humility in Christ.

John 20:12 And she saw two angels in white sitting, one at the head and the other at the feet, where the body of Jesus had lain.

The angels, one at the head and one at the feet, was heaven's affirmation of her position in Christ. A revelation as the head above and not the tail - the angel at the feet, feet- firmly planted in Christ in humility, her humble earthly position, feet on the ground – connection to humanity.

Again Mary Magdalene remembered what Jesus had said and did not leave the tomb.

Luke 8:10 And He said," To you, it has been given to know the mysteries of the kingdom of God..."

John 20:13 Then they said to her woman, why are you weeping?

Mary Magdalene has an encounter and interacts with heaven. At this point, she is caught up between two realms, heaven and earth, and has a dialogue with angels. It is a significant moment as heaven comes down, interacts with earth, unveiling the first mystery of the kingdom of God. She is the first to experience the heavenly and intimate engagement, speaking to heavenly beings. She sees the two angels in white, a glimpse of the purity of heaven where there is no darkness. One angel at the head and the other at the feet where the body of Jesus had lain. And the angel said to her, *"why do you seek Jesus, the living among the dead?"*

"You're right. The tomb is where the dead lie. My Master has risen, He is alive," says Mary Magdalene as she turns and slowly walks away.

Head bowed Mary Magdalene gazed and cleaved to the revelation that the dead no longer lived in tombs, but mumbles to herself, "I do not know where they have laid Him."

John 20:14 Now when she had said this, she turned around and saw Jesus standing there, and did not know that it was Jesus.

John 20:15-18 Jesus said to her, "Woman, why are you weeping? Whom are you seeking?

She supposing Him to be the gardener said to Him,

Sir, if You have carried Him away, tell me where You have laid Him, and I will take Him away."

Jesus said to her, "Mary," Do not cling to Me, For I have not yet ascended to My Father, but go to My brethren and say to them, I am ascending to My Father and your Father and to My God and your God."

He called by her name, and she immediately saw and recognized Him. You may wonder what's in a name. A name is an identifier of knowing who you are in Christ Jesus. People may not know or acknowledge who you are, but He knows you and calls you by name.

Mary Magdalene came and told the disciplines that she had seen the Lord and that He had spoken these things to her.

Once 'Born Again,' 'Do not cling to Me, implies 'GO..' He sends us forth. He says, 'Go' releasing what He has imparted by way of His teachings and His indwelling Spirit within. His blessings, His favor, and every good thing imparted into a believer compel Jesus to be shared. We cannot selfishly hold on His goodness bestowed upon us. We need to release practical and spiritual revelations to a perishing world. The Great Commission is 'Go.' There is a need to move beyond the Teacher and Learner mentality. Ascending to the Father first was an indication that the Holy Spirit would be released to equip believers to do the Father's will. If He is My Father and I say He is your Father, surely you can do the things I did. I say to you, he who believes in Me, the works that I do, he will also do, and greater works will you do as we work together in perfect harmony, *John 14-12 paraphrased.*

FIRST FRUIT ANOINTING/BLESSINGS

Mary Magdalene is the first to receive the realities of heaven;

- The first to experience the revelation of the mysteries of heaven.
- First to rise early – first fruit awakening in the knowledge that putting the things of the kingdom of God first has first fruit benefits. (And everything else will be added unto you)
- The first to come to the tomb.
- First to enter into the spiritual realm and have an encounter with the angels – spoke with the angels
- First to see the resurrected Christ -first to witness life in Christ after death (*I Am the Way, the Truth and the Life, John 14:6a*)
- First to see the Way Maker to the Father (*No one comes to the Father except through Me, John 14: 6b*)
- Mary Magdalene had seven demons that mentally warped her mind – but God still allowed her to be the first to enter into the spiritual realm to witness the existence of the supernatural and the co-working of the two realms.
- Eve transgressed – physically; ate forbidden fruit – spiritually; disobeyed God - but because of God's pre-ordained purpose, she was still able to produce the seed out of whom the lineage of Christ came;
- The woman at the well – flawed physically - her body was misused – God still uses what people perceive as soiled vessels - those whom society frowns down upon to spread the gospel.
- A confirmation that women who have tainted their reputations, the good, the bad, the fallen, etc. are still functional in God's kingdom can still produce good fruit - the God-ordained purpose seed they carry within their spiritual or biological wombs.

12

GODSPEED

Finally, the day for Sasha's departure to leave the country arrived. The girls had promised each other there would be no tears.

"You promised," Sasha gently admonished Veronique trying to hold back her tears.

"It's just the thought of not seeing you for a long time," Veronique sobbed in her friend's arms.

"I'll call every day," said Sasha between sobs.

She knew more tears awaited her in Cape Town. There would be a similar downpour when having to say goodbye to her other friend Linda. She had also promised to spend a couple of days with her before she flew out of the country.

And so began Sasha's venture as she traveled from country to country advocating against human injustice, bridging the inequality divide, motivating women to take their rightful places in society, etc.

13

IN CONCLUSION...

The contents between the pages of this book may arouse and provoke a purpose or destiny awakening for some readers. Although set with an ancient historical backdrop depicting dramatic outcomes, some of the stories allow us to step inside the reality of the critical times we are currently living in. The harsh realities of human suffering and affliction caused by flaws in governing systems can be rectified by those who seek to alleviate injustice and suffering, especially for vulnerable men, women, and children.

To envision as to how they lived in the fervor and sentiments that animated the ancient historical era and the conflicts that either unified or tore them apart, is to capture the environmental and political structure of that period. There is a stark resemblance as to how some of the rulers ruled then and how some of the current rulers of this age rule.

Some great noble minds fought for the betterment of the livelihood of their citizens and the tainted great minds with ulterior motives, for selfish, ambitious gain.

To understand a nation's political administration is to have an insight into its composition and to identify a certain measure of its historical context. A political history molded by passions of greed, conflict, strife corruption, and the desire for power at any cost, is fuelled by an evil spiritual force. The administrators are great men with great minds, but who have become like a dam that overflows beyond its volume (reasoning) capacity — constraining the great mind like a boa constrictor crushing it beyond rational reasoning. The dam gushes forth, breaking its walls and carries off any obstacles that lie in its path. These are rulers who negate to consider the needs of other nations, and it's inhabitants. These are rulers who deny the obligations of their people. These are populist rulers manipulated by the whims of their wealthy citizens. They govern to feed the unquenchable diseased thirst of some of their citizens and the insatiable hunger of the elite for the accumulation of material possessions and wealth. And some rulers stay in power merely to feed their egotistical and narcissistic individualistic selves.

Passions of love, honor, and integrity have also molded and shaped some political histories. These are rulers with great minds who are confronted by the chaotic forces of an unruly river that no one can control or govern. They confront challenges and respond by tapping into their super-powered God-given brains. They are rulers who are their nation's driving force to correct acts of wickedness. Galvanized into action, these great minds utilize their intellectual capacity to its fullest potential. They find solutions to their nations' crises. Are great minds not detached from the most fundamental elements of human life, such as hunger, thirst, and basic human needs. The river flows freely forward when it's banks are broken to find peace and prosperity for its people.

Proverbs 29:2 When the righteous are in authority, the people rejoice; But when a wicked man rules, the people groan.

Social injustices have been meted out and dispensed in its multiple forms of discrimination by states and non-state agencies, causing social disintegration.

The social elite and the untouchables have also contributed to the disintegration of the strong social bonds that communities once enjoyed, because of it's familiarity and safety.

These subtle discrepancies between the middle class, the have's and the have not's, and those who manage to get by have invaded communities. The disparities have driven a wedge between those who live from hand to mouth and those who cannot even afford the basic human living necessities. The vast social inequalities have isolated individuals and communities, bringing along with it the 'rejection stigma.' The unfortunate consequences of these differences have caused some members of the communities to resort to destructive methods of generating an income for survival. But some people genuinely require state intervention. However, a spirit of discernment is needed to distinguish between those who need a helping hand and those who exploit the outstretched hand.

There needs to be a restoration of social community bonds and the collective participation of all the driving sectors within societies. Addressing the indifference, denial of the existence of exclusivity, inequality, and prejudices in the different industries of society is crucial. The procrastination in resolving these issues in the different sectors, ignored and not rectified, is just passed on from generation to generation. These are some of the curses in society that stunt a nation's growth in every sphere. The release of incompetently state-operated enterprises can be steered by competent communities, etc. Such projects will bring along with it a sense of purpose, protection, and pride in the participation of safeguarding the national resources.

People are no longer seeking state 'bailouts.' These bailouts have kept masses in a state of bondage and dependent on the state. In some cases, this has undermined the peoples' sense of responsibility and achievements, thereby inhibiting unrealized and untapped potential. Instead, people seek basic service delivery of rights. These rights bring a sense of dignity, stability into communities, giving the people a meaningful existence and an opportunity to focus on enhancing their own lives and their community.

Psalm 122:7-8b Peace be within your walls (community/nation), and prosperity within your palace(your home/ area of rulership) and peace be within you, (self-worth, dignity, purpose, and self-esteem).

Many predecessors have failed their inhabitants through unkept political promises. Many have pursued ruthless, ambitious drives instead of being steered by moral convictions. Unemployment among many social ills prevails as a dehumanizing and frustrating phenomenon, and poverty remains a global challenge. Unfortunately, some leaders have opted to pursue a personal agenda through selfish ambitious gains. The contest to retain political control is a ruthless desire. Sanctioning biased policies by holding onto office has become the status quo.

However, we see the kaleidoscope for this power now being shaken and pulled down. Societies push back relentlessly against financial greed, partnerships-in-corruption, etc. And, the ground cries out because of the blood spilled on it. Literal bloodshed shed through wars, gangsterism, racial and cultural killings, and God says," Behold a daughter will Arise in your family, in your community, and in your nation, and she shall build my house. God is looking for the building of His house, i.e., his people for they are the temple of the living God.

1 Corinthians 3:16 'Do you not know that you are the temple of God and that the Spirit of God dwells in you.'

Globally women are no longer waiting for man to prioritize their advancement in any social sphere as they change the lives of people. To benefit humanity with some sense of normality, women have turned to their Creator to open doors that no man can open. Having seen and heard the cry of His children, God has honored their request and is causing women to Arise and to take their rightful place in their societies. There's a transformation and reinstating of the dignity of lives as women reach out to the masses. Restoration as created in the image of God with a destiny and purpose, there's hope in recognition of identity.

But with each stand for righteousness, there is a sacrifice to be made. In *2 Samuel 21:8-14* (paraphrased) – we read of the execution of Saul's two sons and five of his grandsons by the Gibeonites. 'But Rizpah, the mother of Sauls two sons and five grandsons from his daughter Merab watches over all of them. She left the comfort of her home and spread the sackcloth on the rock for herself. She prevented vultures from tearing at their bodies during the day and stopped the wild animals from eating them at night; (watchmen on the wall). Watching was from the beginning of the harvest until the late rain poured on them from heaven; (undeterred intercessors) until God released an answer. When King David learned what Rizpah, Saul's concubine had done, he gathered them and had them buried together with the bones of Saul and Jonathan's. After that, God ended the famine in the land of Israel.'

The Lord is a respecter of no persons. He mourns with those who mourn and honors fortitude. The rock Rizpah lay her sackcloth on, is symbolic of the Rock we lay the burdens and the cry of the people. When King David learned what Rizpah had done, he gathered the bones of the dead, did the honorable thing, and buried them. Today, King Jesus, our Rock, has learned what the women who watch over other families/ communities/nations, as well as their own, have done. Having been scattered, He gathers them. The gathering can be geographically, spiritually, psychologically, and emotionally, etc. and raises them from their dead and dry bone situations. Not only does He remove the famine from the lands (absence of the fear of God, natural disasters, etc. - as the Rizpahs' Arise) but He also removes the causes of the famine,
(unrighteousness, spiritual/moral decay, etc.) These are the vultures that tear at the very fiber of the human soul and the wild animals that plunder their dignity, wealth, and resources. They take the bread out of the peoples' mouths, but God gives them a dignified life and purpose for their existence, as 'Women Arise.'

Matthew 25:35-36 'For I was hungry, and you gave Me food; I was thirsty, and you gave me drink; I was a stranger, and you took Me in. I was naked, and you clothed Me; I was sick, and you visited Me; I was in prison, and you came to Me.'

14

POETRY

1 **WE ARE WOMEN**

Made and fashioned in Your likeness,
Molded and shaped into Your image,
 A perfect mirror finish.
But what makes them different?
Is it His love in each with interest
So carefully molded into His image.

Or is it the color of their eyes?
Or the light reflected within?
Or the texture of their hair, it's color, its flair,
Some may ask as they stare.
Is it in the sway of their hips they wonder,
Maybe the shape of their lips, they whisper and ponder.
It can only be the size and contours of their bodies they guess,
Come now, let's stay on par and not digress.

Heads turn when they walk into a boardroom,
They command but never with doom or gloom.
And with subtle control of voice and tone,
They hold and speak into that microphone.

Or maybe the color of their skin, but that's absurd,
That's the last thing, cause it's what makes them unique.
Beauty will fade, so it's not external grandeur,
 But inner beauty, and not provocative demure,
That makes them all priceless women of value,
Worth far more than silver and gold that's true,
 Precious in His sight, that's our Father's view.

I get it; It's the inner strength and power they reflect
A glorious strength, a wonder without defect.
A sense of responsibility to family, communities they willingly accept,
Against injustice, impunity they lament.
Into armed forces against the enemy they defend,
For their loved ones in prayer, they will revenge.

Against inhumane atrocities, they fight,
Inequity, wrongdoing they confront.
Unfailing love and truth, the foundation of what is right,
Righteousness and peace is their delight,
Understanding, and kindness they say, 'a human right.'
Strong and unafraid, the wicked they smite.
Willing to take on the giants of the land,
If it is their cause, you understand.
And in the Spirit they travail,
Against all the odds, they leave a blazing trail.

But as fragile as the wings of a butterfly,
As beautiful as the lilies in the valley,
As gentle as the morning breeze,
Lovely is the intricate creation of them all.

You formed their inward parts,
Your very own Spirit You did impart,
Right from conception, the very start.
Wonderfully and fearfully made,
With Your precious Blood, their price was paid.
They were hidden in You,
As You skilfully wrought their frame,
While In mothers' wombs, You laid claim.
Your eyes saw their substance being yet unformed,
And forever into Your depiction, they were transformed.

How precious are Your thoughts to a woman,
As she tenderly lays in Your bosom.
How great is the sum of them,
Straight from the Rod of Jesse's stem.
Should they be counted,
Matchless ingrained love could never be founded.
They would be more in number than the sand
Because marvelous is the work of Your hand.

Made and fashioned in His likeness,
Molded and shaped into His image,
Is what makes them all women.
Therefore with great abandonment,
Freed from emotional and mental abasement.
Search us, and know our hearts,
You're the One who set us apart.
Try and know our anxieties,
For You are the Three in One Deity.
Remove any wicked ways in us,
Help us to walk in Your enduring trust,
And lead us in the way everlasting.

Made and fashioned in Your likeness,
Molded and shaped into Your image,
Is what makes us all women.

2 TAMED AND UNTAMED TONGUE

The tongue can be a fire,
No bone, but a spitfire.
Defile the entire body,
If uncontrolled, a busybody.

A soft answer turns away wrath from those who hear,
Like honey to the listeners, it's so dear.
A wholesome tongue is a tree of life,
Under whose shadow the listeners hide.

3 A VIRTUOUS WOMAN

She opens her mouth and speaks for the speechless,
She pleads the cause of all who wander in bleakness.
She brings food from afar that will not perish,
And provides the word that they will cherish.
She girds herself with her Master's strength,
Is not afraid of challenges even though intense.

Strength and honor are her clothing,
Sees injustice over her lands, inwardly exploding.
Does not eat the bread of gossip and idleness,
But waits on her Master in humble quietness.
She looks not only to herself and own household
But sees society's plight unfold. It's her responsibility, she's told.

Like Deborah, she rises as a mother to her nation,
When strongmen refused to pay attention,
Instead stood to gain by forming a coalition.
Upon the backs of the fatherless, homeless and widow,
Left them to wander in limbo.

Their greed and power increased,
And their stronghold they would not release,
Unto a woman the Lord His glory would give,
For the sake of His people's peace.

Charm is deceitful, and beauty is passing,
But the women called of the Lord expectations always surpassing.
A woman who fears Him is not afraid,
Cause she knows He'll come to her aid.
She'll be praised by the fruit of her hands,
And her own works will bring her praise,
As to her nations gates,
She brings much-needed maize.
Who can find such a woman?
Seated among you, is that noblewoman.

4 RETURN TO ME

Return to Me and let Me be,
A friend and Father, to you, I'll be.
A fountain of living waters you will see,
You'll never thirst that I guarantee.
Like no other has been to you,
I'll remain forever faithful and true.
I withheld My glory but for a season,
As you ride the storm, you'll see the reason.
Only you have I chosen,
To walk this destiny, I set in motion.
Prepared for you no other can perform,
Cause no other can ride your storm,
Come snow, thunder, or hailstorm.
Each individual uniquely crafted,
Each man in My image grafted.

I've given each his own plan and purpose,
 And with His Blood, My Son has purchased.

Don't leave this earth and say you were never told,
When onto My voice you would not hold,
And instead into others' image, you tried yourself to mold.
Into other shoes, you tried to fit,
And in their destiny, you were a misfit.
I withheld my glory and rain for a moment,
Not to hurt you or be your opponent.
I've clothed you with unfailing strength,
Don't be afraid or keep Me at arm's length.
I've covered you with amazing glory and grace,
You'll shine as My will for you, you embrace.

Endowed with truth and integrity,
An integral part of Me to you.
Strength and power is the fire in your belly,
Burning within you, you can't keep it in,
Release it; you have my permission,
Withholding it, man's deprived of sins remission.
You rank first among My work, Your maker,
For this reason, you were My chosen peacemaker.
Withholding it, you deprive Me of My ingenuity,
My unseen creativity in you, its perpetuity.

Can the trials of the day capture you?
Can My splendor in you lay forever hidden?
Inhibiting temptations of compromise entrapping you
Or the deceits of the accuser of the brethren forever encapsulate
you?
Believe Me when I say, you My cornerstone,
The plans I have for you are yours alone,
Unwrapped the world misses a puzzle piece,
And the genesis for humankind is incomplete.

5 MY BREAKTHROUGH

Overwhelming and persistently they came,
A land of troubled waters covered her head in shame,
A cry of distress, hopelessness in her homestead,
As in captivity, her peace is shattered,
When her sanity to uphold was all that mattered.
Her spirit grows faint within her,
Her heart within dismayed,
As her world lies in disarray.
Overshadowed by grief in her soul,
An unrelenting torrent cannot be consoled.
In a vice grip a vicious hold,
A snare set out to entrap her, I'm told.

Guards besiege her left, right and center,
Day and night cords of torment try to enter.
 Her desperate cries have weakened her resistance;
Adversaries appear too strong in their persistence.
Disaster awaits as darkness sets in her mind to haunt,
To engulf her as anxiety gnaws at her thoughts,
Oppression weighs heavily upon her but is brought to naught,
On her last thread of strength, she has fought.
She clings to You, only You she'll pursue,
Her last ounce of breathe she cries out to you,
Father O' Father, where are You?
Surely You have not forgotten or forsaken me,
Cause I know for a purpose, You created me.

Knitted me together in my mother's womb,
Wonderfully and uniquely You made me bloom.
MY incomplete frame was not hidden from You,
Your eyes saw my unformed body too,

You took pleasure in the completion of me in You.
 Breakthrough, breakthrough,
You are my breakthrough,
When doom and gloom in hot pursuit,
Unceasingly they pursue,
I'm glad in You I took refuge,
Cause You are my breakthrough.
Now in all of life's choices and in all I do,
It's You I'll always choose,
Cause there's none like You,
This, from the very start, I knew.

So I lifted my voice,
You were my only choice,
To You I cried, You shut out the noise.
Weary hands I lifted to You,
Into Your Arms, I flew.
Hoarse and strained vocal cords beseeched Thee,
And now I'm free thanks to Thee.
Breakthrough, breakthrough,
 You are my breakthrough,
Without You what will I do,
I'm glad in You I took refuge.
There is none like You,
None can compare.

You my shield in the days of battle,
You heard my voice through all that rattle.
You held me close,
When in terror I froze,
I could of let go, but me You chose.
 Breakthrough, breakthrough,
You are my breakthrough,
Without You what will I do,
I'm glad in You; I took refuge.

My red and swollen eyes were fixed on You,
You heard my cry. You rescued me,
You are my breakthrough my only breakthrough,
I'm glad in You; I took refuge.

6 MY BROTHER'S KEEPER

A brother, a sister love,
O' that you are like my own sister, my brother,
A child from the womb of my mother,
One who nursed at my mother's breast,
One who's head on her bosom did rest.

I will lead you and bring you into my home,
Now that she no longer has her own,
She who instructed and instilled in me,
Love them as your own, as I loved you.
I will cause you to eat and to drink,
Of the manna, our Father did bring.
And with my hand to lift your head,
When all around you seems to fall instead.
Your right hand will hold and embrace me,
Now aged, others no longer can engage me.

Set them as a seal upon your heart,
A seal like a love song of pure art.
Many waters cannot quench love,
That's as caring and gentle as a dove's.
Nor can the flames of life,
Scorch the embers of strife.
But only a love divine,
Can heal and refine.
Nor can the floods drown its passion,
That a heart the Father has fashioned,

Full of tenderness and compassion.

Live not to regret big brother, big sister,
We have a little sister a little brother,
What shall we do for our sister, our brother?
Who no longer has a mother.
 In the day they are spoken for,
 By the King, they'll be called forth.

If they are a wall, you will build upon them battlements of silver
Understanding, wealth, wisdom and favor be in their quiver,
Bestowed upon them by a mother who took them in.
If they are a door, they'll be enclosed in a mother's protective strength,
Forsake them not into the hands of foreign keepers,
For in their hands, they will be weepers.
But in your home and in their eyes,
 You'll be the one who found them peace.

7   MAN LEVIATHAN

A powerful creature, a man-made beast,
Has this state turned out to be.
But the one I have chosen,
Whose made My kingdom her devotion,
Will outlast his cunning notion for self-promotion.
I'll not fail to speak of her limbs and graceful form,
Each limb and muscle placed in love, a wonder I did perform.
Who dares to strip her of her outer coat,
Without an outward cover, so you could gloat.
But it's her inward beauty I have adorned,
With inner character and dignity, she was born.
Who dares to open their mouth against her comely form,
When in poise she struts in grace, refusing to conform,

Stereotypes say she must be slim to be on any platform,
Misconception, to it, she'll not conform.
When I have ringed her teeth to be fearsome,
Her back a row of shields tightly sealed together,
Strengthened to be the carrier of the young within her.

Each seal a masterpiece,
No ill-fate wind to pass through her with ease,
For with aggression she'll fight for her family's peace
And unity for her nation will never cease.
Her arms outstretched ready to embrace,
Her legs like pillars of marbles to trod the dusty road ahead.
Her sneeze throws out flashes of light,
Her eyes pools reflecting rays ever so bright,
Sees and shines the light beyond the horizon's height.
Firebrand stream from her mouth,
Correction, instruction pour forth for the North and South,
Sparks of fire shoot out all about,
With wisdom," justice is served," she shouts.
Smoke pours out of her nostrils,
With authority, she stills terror and oppression she throttles.
Wrath shoots out at their unbecoming behavior,
As from a boiling pot over a fire of reeds, they'll cry for a Saviour.

Her breathe sets coals ablaze,
Frozen hearts melt, I stand amazed.
Flames dart from her mouth, she's not afraid,
Pride, arrogance, fall before her in disgrace.
Strength resides in her slender neck,
Stretched out graceful, like a turtleneck.
Dismay flees before her in her rage,
Disputes and the debates above injustice she'll not engage.
The folds of her flesh are tightly joined,
Allowing naught of no value to pass through her major points.
Her breasts as hard as rocks, untouched,

Softened by nurturing of her young, they clutched,
A treasure she gives with great pleasure.
When she arises the mighty are terrified,
Submitted to compromise now, they run petrified.
Any hope of subduing her is false,
Any of controlling her is a default.
Cause the mere sight of her is overpowering even for kings,
Especially to those who to wrongdoing cling,
As righteousness with authority justice, she brings.

When she arises, the strong are mystified,
Not knowing what she will decide.
As naked before her, they stand
Having caused all the genocide,
And retreat before her as justice she metes out in her stride.
And the retaliating sword that reaches her has no effect,
Her sharpened reflexes do not defect.
The spear, dart or javelin alike,
Are tossed aside by His Might.
Iron she treats like straw,
And bronze like rotten wood that's been hacksawed.
Arrows do not make her flee,
All try to wear her down, but she laughs with glee,
She stands tall adorned in her royal crown,
Beautiful, we all agree.
Flintstones are like chaff to her,
As they pass through the air in a blur.
A club hurled at her seems like a piece of hay,
 As swiftly with expert timing to one side, she'll sway.
She laughs at the rattling of the lance,
And gives it one haughty glance.
As it lunges forward with a thrust,
With grace and ease, she sidesteps it, in God she trusts.

Her underside are jagged potsherds,

Leaves a trail like a threshing sledge.
She makes the depths churn like boiling cauldron,
Situations characterized by instability and strong emotions she'll not pardon.
She stirs up the sea like a pot of ointment,
Behind her, she leaves a glistening wake,
And before her the earth in devastation quake.
One beside her lifts and places a hedge around her,
One would think the deep has white hair as He surrounds her,
Nothing on earth is her equal when He's around her.

A creature without fear,
When her Maker is near.
She looks down on all who are haughty and proud,
Has learned the humble He uplift and sets apart.
Is queen over all who are arrogant and full of pride,
As in humility and grace, she takes it in her stride.
Praise to the country who her people she holds upright.

About the author

Discontinuing a law degree in pursuit of biblical studies, Cynderella Helen Handwatch graduated with a Bachelor's Degree in Theology in 2000. Finally, with several certificates and diplomas in ministry, she was ordained as Pastor in 2010. Inspired by the Holy Spirit, she now skilfully incorporates her biblical knowledge and insight in her writings. Born and raised in South Africa, she currently resides in New Zealand.

OTHER TITLES BY THE AUTHOR

HIS EYE UPON US

Destined to meet under horrific circumstances, is an intriguing story of five young girls. But a glorious future filled with promises and hope transforms their lives.

Sasha: The oldest child of a struggling single mother, hopes to improve the lot of her family by venturing off on an exciting career but instead is ensnared into a Human Trafficking syndicate. In a do-or-die situation, and despite overwhelming challenges, she maintains her integrity by holding fast to her Christian faith and is strong enough to believe it will pull her through.

Veronique: Abducted from her village and caught in the vicious web of the Human Trafficking underworld, spurred by her newfound faith and the power of a Spirit much higher and stronger than her own is her tenacity to survive. The experience is the discovery of a purpose-ordained calling in Christ Jesus.

Linda: Born in the comfort of family wealth but determined to make it on her own, sets off and finds happiness, love, and friendship from an unlikely source. She returns home determined to break the family's racial bondage and religious compromise. The reform almost costs her the loss of her fiancé and alienation from her loved ones. But she discovers a superior destiny and realizes she is prepared to sacrifice everything to fulfill this calling.

Angel: Betrayed by her uncle and sold into the cutthroat world of Human Trafficking. An ex-client turned Good Samaritan rescues her restoring her faith. She becomes a renowned producer/choreographer and a human rights activist. She brings justice for the exploited poor and reminds them that God has not turned a blind eye.

Reanna: A beautiful and alluring woman turns villain for money and material possessions, but beneath the offensive behavior is a borderline identity disorder and a cry for real love, a cry to be released from the Human Trafficking netherworld. Found in the most incredible places are escape and forgiveness.

The Garden Tea Party

An anthology of poems by Cynderella Helen Handwatch illustrated with gardens created and photographed by Elisabeth Hester Bayly as a fundraising project to fight against human trafficking, abuse against women and children, and all forms of injustices against humanity.

INTENT AND PURPOSE

While the published books used as fundraising tools, they are also platforms to engage and mobilize readers to a partnership, collaboration, networking with the cause of transforming lives. Contributions can be in prayer, time, deed, in progressive and positive concepts, and dialogue.
We are appreciative of any form of positive interaction.

The following accounts hold any monetary, donations/funding deposits;

The Nehemiah Building Project (NBP)
Account No: 38 9020 0094674 00
Type: Cheque Account
Swift Code: CITINZ 2XX
Kiwi Bank- New Zealand
Contact email: chandwatch@gmail.com

Umgeni Community Empowerment Centre (UCEC)
Account No: 4058046503
Type: Cheque Account
Branch Code; 630326
Intl Dep Branch Code: 632005
Swift Code: ABSAZAJJ
Absa Bank- South Africa
Contact email: gloria@ucec.org.za

Website: www.ucec.org.za
0800 RESCUE
+27 318247951/7961

www.ingramcontent.com/pod-product-compliance
Lightning Source LLC
Chambersburg PA
CBHW051952060726
47506CB00011B/787